小樹系列

Little Trees

中英對照

周圍都是您的貴人

Helpers All Around

林幸惠——著

湯耀洋——英譯校訂

身邊都是你的貴人

　　五年前幸惠師姊寫了《心光有愛：映照生命的幽谷》，讓我有機會跟隨送書到花東、宜蘭、台北等七所監獄，在和典獄長及教誨師交流當中，第一次感受到「地藏王菩薩」的願力和苦心，在這些獄政工作者的身上體現的再恰當不過。

　　因此也激發了我們小小的願力，希望有機會能把台灣島內的五十一所監獄、看守所都走一趟。

　　三年的疫情，這世界的改變太大了，為了能保住生命健康的最後一道防線，隔離再隔離，非常不容易，三年撐過去了，世界秩序的混亂才正開始：天災，人禍，戰爭……等。國內金融詐騙，吸毒、販毒到處都是，學校因招不到學生而關閉，有典獄長告訴我們，他們還在擴建牢房！

這期間，有人說，還是疫情比較好，一切活動停止，哪裡都去不了，生活回歸純樸，連地球空氣也變好了。所有的人都戴著口罩，連感冒生病的人也少了。

長期關注社會問題的幸惠師姊，借用口罩的功能，把人性本善的想法，加上過去輔導個案的實際經歷故事，又寫了《魔法口罩＠未來事件簿》一書。

我們繼續以這本書和監獄、看守所及偏鄉離島的中學生結緣——邀請這些同學在閱讀該書後，把心得寫下來。為了鼓勵他們閱讀、寫心得，我們也給用心的同學頒發獎金。

每次在他們的閱讀心得中發現：一本書的力量，因為書中一句話、一個故事，喚醒了這些沉迷在迷宮而走不出去的受刑學員，他們在書中找到答案，找到他們的真如本性，懺悔過去的錯誤行為，發願再回到社會一定會發善心，行善事。我想，證嚴上人要我們做淨化人心的事，這算是第一步。

有位典獄長感慨地說，有很多同學在期滿出去前，都發願重返社會後一定要做一個正當的人；但可惜沒多久有些人又回來了！其中有很多是吸毒和販毒的人，原因是他們出去找不到適當的工作，社會上的人若用特別的眼光看待他們，就會讓他們慢慢又失去自信心，在迷惘中，禁不起誘惑的他們，往往很快就走回頭路了！

所以，重點在這些更生人回到社會時，我們能不能給他們機會，順手拉他們一把，成為他們生命中的貴人。

回想個人過去踏入社會的成長過程中，有很多重要的關頭，也都是因為遇見貴人、獲得相助，才順利解決困難的問題。

記得三十年前，我的工廠準備要接一個美國名牌的訂單，但要接這張單，工廠必須經過嚴格的驗廠認證，我們完全沒經驗，更不知從何做起，正在傷腦筋時，恰巧在飛機上同排座位，遇到三十年不見的高中同學，他竟然是這家美國公司的驗廠審查專員，結果如何就不必細說，當然經過指導順利過關。

疫情期間經常在鄉下老家隔離，發現故鄉人口老化，年輕人外流，母校面臨合併廢校！我發願要為故鄉做地方創生，開始組織農民栽種可可樹，然而這些可可樹要三年才能有成果，農民三年沒有收入怎麼辦？台大農學院教授指導我要發展林下經濟，還在苦思中，我朋友介紹有一個專家在培育可以在樹下離地栽培的薑苗，可以找他接洽，見面交換名片，第一時間被認出來，又是五十年不見的高中同學，是農業改良場退休的專家，現在自己成立種苗培育中心。天啊！我不懂農業，只是發了一個願，農業專家的同學就出現了，現在是我可可合作社的工作伙伴。

最近因為出國十多天，把車停在離機場很近的師姊家車庫，回來開車時才發現輪胎破了，自己換上備胎，結果發現備胎也沒氣。當天是星期天，所有輪胎行都休息，只能打電話給道路救援，結果是要求出場費一千二百元，維修費另計。重點是他們手上有工作，多久來不知道，我和家人已經在路邊等了一個小時。這時有位年輕婦人騎單車經過，見到我們的窘狀，即刻給我們一個維修師傅的電話，還說：這師傅人很好，他一定可以幫你們的。我們馬上打電話，師傅客氣地說，我人在外面，要回店裡拿工具，你們要等一下喔！沒多久，師傅來了，快速的把兩個沒氣的輪胎都修好了，只要四百元，我不好意思想多給二百元，師傅卻堅持不要，還說不好意思，讓你們久等了。

所以說，我們隨時都需要貴人相助，當然我們自己也要期許隨時成為別人的貴人。

這次，幸惠師姊再出書《周圍都是您的貴人》，是要告訴我們：「身邊都是你的貴人」。我想，她的用意是要給迷惘的人多一份信心，只要發善心，與人結好緣，身邊到處都是你的貴人。在書出版前，末學榮幸先睹並寫下小序，希望自己也能成為別人的貴人。感恩！

　　　　　江智超（彰化縣可可蔬果生產合作社理事主席，慈濟志工）

周圍的貴人

　　前幾天去超市，因颱風天多買了一些糧食，排了很長的隊伍，好不容易輪到我結帳時，突然找不到錢包，很焦急地在大包包裡翻找了好幾分鐘，後面排隊的一位婦人居然跟我說，「慢慢找不急，再想一下，就會找到的。」頓時感覺一股溫暖湧上來，回頭向她致謝；這樣不顧自己的利益，只想幫助別人冷靜下來的心意，讓我很感動，也感染了我，下次去買東西時，遇到慌亂的人，我也要學會說「慢慢來不急，再想一下，就會找到的。」甚至於上公車時，有人卡裡餘額不足，我就幫他付現，這是那位以善感染我的婦人，帶給我的善效應。

　　現在的推銷真是五花八門，行銷像亂槍打鳥般地打電話，讓人很干擾，很受不了。有一天，我跟銀行的業務經理正談話時，她接到一通好像也是銀行業務員的行銷電話，只聽到她不慌不忙地說：「對不起我們是同行，請你不用浪費時間跟我解說，多把時間拿去向別人行銷吧。如果客戶有需要，我們也可以互相交流介紹喔。」讓人感覺好有人文素養。她說現在銀行業務式微，體諒他們的辛苦，不需要惡語相向，免得彼此情緒都受到影響。我因此又學到了一招：為了不影響各自的情緒，接到行銷電話時千萬不要不耐煩，即便要拒絕對方，也要有禮貌的拒絕。

　　我天生個性就愛幫助別人，但有時候儘管是出於好意，卻不一定適合每個情況。有時候會被誤解成不諒解的惡意，這是我屢次遭遇到的窘境。我的好朋友，已有很乖巧的三個小孩，但因老公婚外情，讓她困擾多年，常聽她抱怨，作為她的朋友，我是多年忠誠的傾聽者，有一次她的老公很過分，還把小三帶去醫院探望婆婆，她的婆婆也很開心地接受小三的貴重禮物，她知道後更加傷心難過，埋頭在我肩上直哭，說自己帶三個小孩很辛苦，婆婆居然見利忘義，不顧多年的情分，我也義憤填膺地勸她：「那就離婚吧，沒什麼值得留戀啦！」沒想到，她居然抬起頭來有點嗔怒地說：「我們這麼多年朋友，妳一點都不了解我。」就回家了，然後好幾個月都不跟我聯絡，我很沮喪，不知道哪裡犯錯，後來去找心理諮商師才知道，他人是不可以幫當事者做決定的，即使建議是出於好意，卻讓好友認為，我無法體會她的感受與支持她的選擇。我終於了解到自己的錯失，於是認真去讀心理諮商。

　　事後回想，好友確實是我的貴人，她讓我有機會反思和改進自己。未來再遇到類似情況時，或許可以選擇更多地傾聽和支持，讓朋友知道我是在乎她的感受和選擇，而不是直接給出建議。這樣既能保護朋友間的友情，也能更好地幫助人，因為她的事讓我也學習而成長很多。我跟她道謝與道歉後，我們回復了原本的好交情。

　　現代人正面對一個巨變的時代，舊的知識正被加速淘汰，而新的知識也時刻不斷誕生，學習已經沒有一步到位或一勞永逸這回事，而是隨時穿插在人們的人生旅途中。我們就彷彿在風暴中前行，而學習就是我們前進的羅盤，也是我們安度前方任何風暴的唯一指引。

請珍惜身邊人的緣分，感恩每件事的正面意義，而且能激起學習的動機，並培養自主學習能力，才能應對未來變動的適應和解決能力。

　　感恩並深切地祝福每一位讀者，都可以看清所有事件中的貴人，並得到學習，而成為別人的貴人。人生永遠學不完，我們都在一艘滿載陽光的船上乘風破浪。

　　　　　　　　　　　　　　　　林幸惠（本書作者）

Introduction   14

1. The line between good and evil   16

2. Adversity is a touchstone of life   48

3. Loss and grief   92

4. Things happened to protect you   124

5. Be your own cheerleader   154

6. Surprises after the river bend   190

7. Are you my buddy?   238

8. In our later years   274

目次

推薦序
身邊都是你的貴人　　江智超　　　　　　2

作者序
周圍的貴人　　　　　　　　　　　　　8

引　子　　　　　　　　　　　　　　　14

一、誤解與善的距離　　　　　　　　16

二、逆境是人生試金石　　　　　　　48

三、失落的哀傷情緒　　　　　　　　92

四、事件是來保護你的　　　　　　124

五、當自己的啦啦隊　　　　　　　154

六、柳暗花明的轉角　　　　　　　190

七、誰是好朋友？　　　　　　　　238

八、老後的時光　　　　　　　　　274

後序
吸毒一次，貽害一世　　鐘炯元　　302

In my previous book, The Magic Mask at The Registry of Future Events, the protagonist Xiaoshu, through Magician Abo and the Magic Mask, experienced many events and also helped many people around him. Xiaoshu has learned a lot and changed a lot from this experience. At the end of the book, both Magician Abo and the Magic Mask vanished. Although by that time Xiaoshu had realized that many problems in the world must be resolved only by his own positive attitude and empathy, what made him saddest was that he would never again see Magician Abo, his guardian angel. Going forward, he, himself, would have to resolve all his own problems in life, however thorny they may be.

When our guardian angel is gone, how do we handle it? Can we find our own guardian angel? From here, the story of this book shall develop.

前作《魔法口罩＠未來事件簿》中，主角少年小樹透過神奇阿伯與魔法口罩，在經歷許多事件的同時，也幫助了周遭很多人。經過許多歷練，讓小樹懂得許多、也改變很多。故事最終，神奇阿伯和魔法口罩都消失了！儘管小樹這時已體會到，人世間的許多問題，要靠自己正向的諒解去尋求解答，但他最難過的還是生命中的貴人神奇阿伯不再現身，往後遇到難題都只能靠自己。

當貴人不在，我們要如何自處？可以自己去找尋生命中的貴人嗎？本書故事，由此開展……

第一章
CHAPTER 1

誤解與善的距離

The line between good and evil

Xiaoshu has become dispirited and depressed since the Magic Mask Abo disappeared, and for a long time he has been unable to find the energy to do anything. However, his own experience has made it very clear in his heart that whatever he does, nothing gives him as much joy as helping others.

One day, team leader Wu called on everyone to clean up the beach, but Xiaoshu was in no mood for it. Wu said, "Wang Xiaofang in our volunteer team is feeling low. It's a good thing to clean up the beach together, and you can also at the same time spend time with her to take her mind off her troubles."

"What is her problem? I have zero experience in emotional matters, so I guess I can't help her."

Without Magician Abo and the Magic Mask, Xiaoshu seems totally lost and suddenly disoriented. He can't even deal with his own affairs, so how can he be expected to help others?

"Xiaofang's boyfriend dumped her but she liked him. Her new boyfriend was too cosseting or even controlling–like a helicopter parent, and that annoyed her very much. She wants to see the ocean and take a breather, so beach cleaning is just the thing for her," said Wu.

話說小樹自從魔法口罩阿伯消失了以後，變得若有所失且鬱鬱寡歡，很長一段時間都提不起勁來。不過種種經歷讓他內心很清楚，無論做什麼事都沒有助人來得快樂。

　　有一天，吳小隊長拉著大家一起去海邊淨灘，小樹本來沒什麼動力，但小隊長說：

　　「我們志工隊的王小芳遇到了感情困境。一起淨灘是好事，順便還可以陪她散散心。」

　　「是哪方面的問題？我對感情的事並沒有經驗，應該幫不上忙吧？」

　　沒了神奇阿伯和魔法口罩，小樹彷彿失去手腳、頓失方向，自己都是泥菩薩過江了，哪還能幫別人！

　　「小芳被喜歡的男友拋棄，後來新交男友又對她緊迫盯人，她感到很煩，想出來看海散心。淨灘活動對她來說剛好！」小隊長說。

So, Xiaoshu and his group set off to the beach to clean up. Seeing the youngsters pick up garbage, many tourists took pictures, and some gave the activity thumbs up. Near the end of the clean-up, Wang Xiaofang shouted, "Ouch, my fingers were pierced by broken glass!"

Xiaoshu quickly took the first aid kit and carefully disinfected and bandaged her.

Sighing, Xiaofang said, "I must have been distracted by those annoying relationship things and broken glass pricked me."

Xiaoshu said, "What is it that upset you so much that you lost your attention and got hurt?"

"It's a long story!" Xiaofang paused to think for a while, and continued: "My ex-boyfriend and I had been dating for three years, but out of the blue without any reason, he broke up with me. I was very sad, but I wanted to get a new boyfriend ASAP in the hope that the new guy may soothe my sorrow and fill the emptiness so I could forget the old wounds. But I didn't expect that my new boyfriend would turn out to be even worse. The new boyfriend is even more annoying. He feels he's always right, and he also tracks my whereabouts all day long. I really can't stand him, and I want to break it up, but he begged and

於是，小樹一夥人整裝出發到海邊淨灘。許多遊客看到他們幾位同學在撿垃圾，有人拍照、有人豎起大拇指比讚。在垃圾快撿完時，突然聽到王小芳大叫「我的手被玻璃割到了！」

　　小樹聞聲，動作飛快取來急救箱，細心地幫她消毒包紮。

　　小芳嘆氣：「應該是我無法甩掉煩人的事，心不在焉，才會不小心被玻璃割到吧？！」

　　小樹邊消毒邊關心問道：「是什麼事讓你心煩到失神受傷呢？」

　　「說來話長！」小芳話稍停，想了一下，繼續說：「我和前男友已交往三年，他竟然不管一切就提分手，沒來由就離我而去！讓我很難過。後來就想趕快再交一個新男友，希望能填補遺憾和空虛，讓我忘卻舊傷，沒想到結果更慘！這一個更讓人心煩，除了自以為是，還整天疑神疑鬼追蹤我的行動，我真的受不了，想說分手

pleaded and tracked me even more rigorously than before. That really drives me up the wall. I have no idea how to proceed." The more Xiaofang spoke, the more distressed she became, and her face showed it.

"You will have to talk it over with him. Perhaps, your boyfriend, deep down, feels highly uncertain about your relationship," Xiaoshu figured, "Maybe you need to talk to a psychotherapist; maybe that will be helpful for the two of you. If necessary, I can connect you with my cousin Anli, the 'Smiling Anli', a relationship and emotion-focused therapist. She may be able to help." Xiaoshu suddenly remembered his cousin Anli, whom he hadn't seen in the longest time.

"Smiling Anli…I've heard the name. Okay, I'll seek her out when I have time."

Xiaoshu suddenly thought of Magician Abo who had given him a magic mask. The thought made Xiaoshu downbeat. He lowered his head and sighed, "I used to know an older but magical friend who had taught me a lot of things at critical moments in my life. He taught me to see things from different perspectives and viewpoints, but unfortunately this good friend is no longer with me, and I miss him dearly."

算了，但他又苦苦哀求，而且更加緊迫盯人，這讓我更煩了，不知道該怎麼辦？」小芳愈說愈苦惱，整個眉頭都糾在一起了。

「這必須要你們兩個好好談一談。或許，你男友背後有不為人知的巨大不安感吧？」小樹判斷，「也許要找心理諮商師聊聊，對你們或許都會有幫助。若有需要，我可以介紹我表姊給你認識，她叫『微笑安莉』，是情感跟情緒的心理諮商師，也許幫得上忙喔。」小樹突然想起好久不見的安莉表姊。

「微笑安莉！我聽過她的名字喔。好，那請你幫我介紹，我有空就去找她。」

講到這，小樹突然想起給他魔法口罩的神奇阿伯，鬱悶的他低下頭來感嘆說道：

「我之前認識一個神奇的忘年之交，他總在關鍵時刻教我很多事，讓我學會從不同角度與立場去思考，可惜這個好朋友已經不在了，我很懷念他。」

Hearing Xiaoshu's outpouring of emotion, Xiaofang quietly held his hand, thanked him for attending to her wound, and said, "Perhaps it is predestined whether two people will get along. You miss this magician friend in much the same way I miss my ex-boyfriend: I think of him in the dead of night, and I miss him even more so in the noise of a city. I just can't keep his images from showing up in my mind. I just can't let go of those reminisces." She was sobbing.

At this time, the team leader, standing not far away, urged everyone to assemble.

"We've come to clean the beach as well as to cleanse our hearts. Pack up and throw away the filthy worries in our hearts, and stare at the vastness of the ocean to make our hearts more tolerant of any kind of people and accept all sorts of uncertain things in the world." What the team leader said just seemed to address what had been bothering Xiaoshu and Xiaofang at the moment. "When we're packed, let's watch the sea together!" The team leader proposed.

After packing up the garbage, everyone sat on the beach and looked at the sunset; the red setting sun in the sky was reflected on the surface of the sea. The sight of the sea and the sky exhilarated everyone.

小芳聽到小樹的心聲，默默地握住他的手，謝謝他的細心包紮並說道：「人與人之間相處的緣分，也許是有定數的吧。你這樣不就跟我想念前男友一樣，夜深人靜也想，吵雜鬧市更想，就是無法清除掉他的影像，對過去的種種回憶總是無法割捨！」小芳低下頭來拭淚。

　　這時，小隊長在不遠處催大家集合：

　　「來淨灘也是來淨心的，把內心不乾淨的煩惱打包丟掉，看看大海的遼闊，我們的心量就能更寬大地包容任何人，接納世間種種不確定的事。」小隊長講的這些，剛好契合小樹和小芳此刻心境。「等收拾好，我們一起去看海吧！」小隊長提議。

　　收拾好打包垃圾，大家就坐在沙灘上，望著西沉夕陽，紅彤彤的落日和揮灑在天際的晚霞映照海面，海天一色的景致讓人心情舒暢極了。

A few days afterwards, Xiaoshu had nothing on his calendar, so he flipped through his old photos, not looking for anything in particular. He thought about how he used to play with his cousins when he was a child. He also thought about how he had followed the instructions of Magician Abo to get his relatives and friends out of a bind; he wondered how they were doing. He just mentioned Anli to Xiaofang, so it seems that it was a good time to visit cousin Anli.

Xiaoshu rummaged through the photos looking for the ones with Anli's cousin in them. When he stared at the photos, his feet felt a sudden and inexplicable sharp pain. The pain was clear and very intense, and he intuitively felt that the pain probably had something to do with cousin Anli. He put down the album and quickly dialled cousin Anli.

As soon as the call went through, Xiaoshu heard Anli's cry as she started to talk: "My foot hurts a lot; maybe it's broken! I'm scared to death. What should I do? Did God send you to save me?"

"Cousin, I'm Xiaoshu! What happened to you?"

"I was hit by a car and that vehicle ran off. My foot is injured. I'm lying in a low-lying area by the river, totally unable to move and out of people's sight. What should I do?"

幾天後，小樹閒來無事隨手翻起了舊照片，他惦念著小時候玩在一起的堂表兄弟姊妹們，不知道那些遭逢困境時靠著小樹在魔法口罩阿伯指示下解除危機的親友們現在可好？尤其不久前才跟小芳提到，好像該去看看安莉表姊了。

　　小樹特地翻找出有安莉表姊的照片，當凝視照片時，他的腳突然感到一陣莫名劇痛，那個痛清楚且強烈，讓他直覺恐怕與表姊有關。他急忙放下相簿，趕緊撥電話給安莉表姊。

　　電話一通，傳來安莉哭泣的聲音，只聽她哽咽說道：「我的腳好痛，可能骨折啦！我好害怕，怎麼辦呀？你是老天派來救我的嗎？」

　　「表姊，我是小樹啦！你發生什麼事了？」

　　「我被車撞了，肇事車輛已逃逸無蹤！我的腳受傷，現在躺在河邊的低窪地，動彈不得，也沒人發現我，該怎麼辦？」

"Give me your exact location, and I'll call an ambulance to rescue you, okay?" Xiaoshu said to her while thinking to himself, "what a coincidence!" As he looked back, he remembered that when he was a child, cousin Anli loved to fight for the disadvantaged people when she saw injustice, and she was honest and ready to help, although she also loved to lecture others.

At the emergency room of the hospital, cousin Anli told Xiaoshu that fortunately she had suffered only minor injuries. The two of them had not seen each other for a long time. She asked, "It's amazing. Why did you happen to call me at that time, when I needed help?" As Xiaoshu was thinking about how to answer, Anli continued, "Actually, we have all heard that you have magical power, and have saved many people from disasters. Is it true?"

"It's nothing. They are all coincidental."

Having said that, Xiaoshu did feel deep down that, even without the magic mask and Magician Abo, he himself still seemed to possess some sort of sensing power, which could be used to help others. Frankly, he felt excited just thinking about it.

「告訴我出事地點，我趕緊叫救護車去救你，好嗎？」小樹心想，事情怎麼會這麼巧？！同時想起小時候，印象中的表姊最愛打抱不平，正直又熱心，但也愛教訓人。

　　到了醫院急診室探視表姊，幸好只是皮外傷並無大礙。久違的表姊一見到小樹就問：「太神奇了吧，你怎麼會剛好在這個時候打電話給我？」小樹正思索該如何回答，表姊接著說：「其實我們都聽說了，你有神奇的魔法，幫很多人度過災難，這是真的嗎？」

　　「沒什麼啦，巧合而已。」

　　雖這麼說，但小樹心裡確實感受到，即便沒有了魔法口罩和阿伯，他似乎仍然有某種感應能力，甚至可以用來幫助別人，想想還真令人興奮呢。

"You look so handsome; are you seeing anyone special?" cousin Anli asked, cutting off his thoughts in a heartbeat.

"No. Why?"

"I'd bet a lot of girls are vying for your affection."

Xiaoshu smiled awkwardly and said, "I'm not interested! I don't want a girlfriend. That is too much trouble. I haven't finished my studies yet. And I have always felt that women are difficult to understand, and I don't want to understand them." In fact, Xiaoshu doesn't talk about feelings because his mind is clear about this matter, and he remembers that Magician Abo once told him, "You should enrich yourself as much as you can when you are young. Once you get involved in relationships and feelings, you have to spend time and effort. Be careful not to be tangled by feelings until you're mentally mature. Be sure to invest more in yourself while you are still young. A lot of responsibilities are awaiting you in the future!"

"I guess you haven't met anyone you like yet, right? Would you like me to hook you up with someone?" Anli asked.

"No and no. I really don't want to be in a relationship yet at this time. I think it's wonderful to be single. Less burdensome," Xiaoshu replied categorically.

"Sounds like you're anti-love?"

「長得這麼帥，有女朋友了嗎？」熱心的表姊劈頭就問，瞬間打斷他的思緒。

　　「沒有呀，怎麼了？」

　　「一定有很多女孩子追你喔！」

　　小樹尷尬地笑說：「我沒有興趣啦！也沒想要找女朋友，太麻煩了，學業還沒完成，總覺得女人很難懂，也不想懂啦！」小樹不談感情，因為心中清澈如水，記得魔法口罩阿伯曾跟他說：「年輕時應該多充實自己。一旦要談感情，你就得投入時間和心力，在心智和年齡都尚未成熟之前，要謹慎不要被情困住。趁年少多投資自己，將來還有很多責任要承擔！」

　　「應該是還沒遇到喜歡的人吧？要不要幫你介紹啊？」表姊追問。

　　「不是啦，也不需要，我目前是真的還不想談戀愛。我覺得一個人過日子也很好，沒有負擔。」早熟的小樹斬釘截鐵地回答。

　　「看來你對戀愛有冷感症？」

Xiaoshu smiled but said nothing while a friend visiting cousin Anli interjected, "Nice-looking guys don't want to have girlfriends. It's no wonder many girls can only choose to be single."

Cousin Anli quickly made the introduction: "She is a colleague of mine, and she is interning as a psychotherapist."

Xiaoshu and the interning psychotherapist exchanged polite greetings, and cousin Anli, accompanied by her colleague, was about to return home to recuperate. Xiaoshu left first, though.

A few days later, cousin Anli called to thank Xiaoshu, but she also said something that made Xiaoshu break out in a cold sweat, "There's something about you that I don't know if I should tell you."

"Just say it. I am hiding nothing," Xiaoshu said with a smile.

"I've already resolved it for you, but I want to let you know so you can keep an eye out for it."

"Sounds quite serious. What's it?"

"Do you know Wang Xiaofang?"

"Yes, she's my classmate in elementary school. What's wrong?"

"Are you guys close?"

"Not particularly."

小樹微笑不語，表姊身旁剛來探望她的朋友也插話：「帥哥都不想交女朋友了，難怪許多女生都只能選擇單身啦！」

　　表姊趕緊介紹：「她是我的同事，目前在接受諮商心理師的實習訓練。」

　　兩人禮貌性的互相打招呼後，表姊在同事陪伴下準備返家休養，小樹就先離開了。

　　隔沒幾天，表姊打電話來，除了感謝小樹，還說了一件讓小樹嚇出一身冷汗的事：

　　「有一件跟你有關的事，不知道該不該告訴你？」

　　「您就說呀，我應該沒有不可告人的祕密吧。」小樹笑笑地說。

　　「我是已經幫你解決了啦，但想說還是要告知你，讓你提防一下。」

　　「什麼事呀？聽起來好像很嚴重。」

　　「你認識王小芳嗎？」

　　「認識呀，她是我小學同學，怎麼了？」

　　「你跟她很要好嗎？」

　　「一般而已啦。」

"Have you gone out with her recently and had pictures taken together?"

"Have we?" Xiaoshu thought for a moment, "Oh, we met a while back at a beach cleanup. But I don't remember having our pictures taken. What's wrong?"

"Xiaofang's boyfriend saw a photo of you two together, you holding her hand, so he thought that you were Xiaofang's new boyfriend."

"OMG. He's got it all wrong. Xiaofang injured her hand while picking up garbage at the beach, so I helped her bandage it, and we talked a little. We hadn't seen each other in ages. People at the event took pictures here and there, so I didn't pay attention. There isn't any intimacy. This is a misunderstanding spinned out of control. I didn't even know there was such a thing!"

"This young man–Wang Xiaofang's new boyfriend–is looking everywhere for you. Whenever he meets people, he asks them who you are, and says he wants to teach you a lesson. Fortunately, the psychotherapist friend of mine who visited me at the hospital happened to be the man's sister. When she saw the photo and realized that it was you that her brother was looking for, she quickly brought her brother to me. I still

「你是不是最近有跟她一起玩，還合照過？」

「有嗎？」小樹想了想，「喔，前陣子大家相約，一起參加了淨灘活動。但我不記得有拍照，怎麼了嗎？」

「小芳的男友看到你跟她的合照，只見你牽著她的手，讓他以為你是小芳新交的男友……」

「天哪，誤會大了，她是在淨灘時不小心手受傷，我好心幫她包紮，稍微聊了一下。我們很久沒見面了，現場大家都隨意拍照，我也沒留意，哪有什麼親密關係啦，這誤會也太誇張了，我都不知道有這種事！」

「這個男的還到處找你，逢人就問你是誰，説要給你一點教訓。還好，上次來醫院探望我的同事，碰巧就是他的姊姊，她看到照片發現是你，就趕緊帶她弟弟來

remember the first time we met, he looked fiercely angry, as if the whole world owes him money, and he showed me a photo of you holding Xiaofang's hand."

Looking at the photo that Anli had just texted him, Xiaoshu knew that he had been terribly wronged. It's all about the angle of the camera, right? He had no idea where this photo had come from. He felt that he had been set up. After the phone call, he rushed to find Anli to sort out the situation in her presence.

"My psychotherapist friend and her brother were raised by their mother alone since they were little, and their mother often complained about her ex-husband for not being responsible. Her frequent complaints have invariably changed the personality of her two children. The boy has become insecure and had difficulty controlling his own negative emotions, which was a sequelae of his childhood trauma. He believed that Xiaofang had originally liked him, but she has kept asking to break up with him. She changed her mind because she had a new boyfriend. He believes that hurting the other man is a sign of loyalty to Xiaofang. He also believes that he can also threaten her not to 'mess around' in the future. But this is actually a self-centered and totally wrong idea." Anli

找我。我還記得初見面，對方面帶凶氣怒目相向的樣子，好像全世界的人都對他不起，他當場給我看你牽小芳手的合照。」

看著表姊傳來照片，小樹心想，這也太冤了！這根本是拍攝角度的問題吧？也不知這照片哪來的？心中有種被栽贓的感覺！結束與表姊的電話，他拔腿飛奔去找表姊，要當面理清原委。

「她們姊弟從小就由母親單獨扶養長大，母親常怨恨離婚父親的不負責任，無形就把情緒帶給姊弟倆，所以這個男生有極度的不安全感，很難控制負面的情緒，這是童年創傷後遺症。他認為小芳本來是喜歡他的，後來一直吵著要分手，一定是因為有了新歡。他認為去傷害對方，就是對小芳忠誠的表現，還可以威脅她以後不要『亂來』。但這其實是自以為是的錯誤想法。」表姊

stopped talking to have a drink of water while Xiaoshu was dumbfounded. She continued:

"I told him that when a flower blooms, butterflies will come naturally. Romantic feelings are nurtured not by not threat, but by attraction. A cactus can hardly attract people to pet it! People should cultivate and improve themselves, which is a better way to attract others. If the love is gone, you must leave the relationship with equanimity and amiability like a gentleman. Once you lose, remember to let go, give yourself blessings, and the next relationship will be better."

Agreeing with Anli, Xiaoshu said, "Yes! Hurting an opponent–or even an imaginary one–is the worst option. Not only will it bring serious consequences, but it may also lead to criminal prosecution and lawsuits. Furthermore, it will make the other person, who no longer loves you, stay further away and less inclined to approach you again."

Nodding, Anli said, "This boy is very smart. I talked to him for two hours, but I felt that he was still enveloped by inexplicable anxiety which he didn't know how to shake off. I told him that usually a person can survive a trauma without his body knowing it, so if he runs into a little more stimulation, the old wound may resurface again. The biggest anxiety of people

停下話喝口水，小樹已聽得目瞪口呆。她繼續說：

「我跟他說，花若盛開蝴蝶自來，感情是吸引來的，不是威脅來的。如果是一株仙人掌，肯定很難吸引人碰觸它吧！人應該要自我培養提升，才是吸引對方更好的方法。如果愛沒了，轉身一定要漂亮，這才是君子風度。一旦失去，要謹記放下，給自己祝福，下一個會更好。」

小樹很認同表姊的觀點：「對！傷害對手——甚至可能只是假想敵——是最壞的選擇，不只後果嚴重，還可能背負刑責、吃上官司！而且會讓已經不再愛你的對方躲得更遠，更不敢接近你。」

表姊點點頭：「這男生很聰明。我跟他談了兩個鐘頭，但感覺他還是被莫名的焦慮所籠罩，不知怎樣才能擺脫。我就跟他講，通常創傷過了，人也挺下來了，但我們的身體可能還不知道，所以若再遇到一點刺激就可

comes from distrust, and what this boy really doesn't trust is actually himself. Maybe he is running away from himself, from the major traumatic events of his past, and his true emotions are still suppressed in the depths of his consciousness.

"So what should we do?" Xiaoshu said. He had already gotten very involved in the situation and he was getting worried about the man.

"I have made another appointment with him, and we will use reversion and trauma therapy to explore his anxiety and help him further. Fortunately, he probably won't want to bother you anymore," cousin Anli said. "Many young people can't come to terms with the frustration of breaking up, so intuitively they vent their anger in a destructive way and they threaten the other party. They don't realize that their actions will only drive their former lovers farther away, help them validate their decision to break up, and make them regret not having broken up their relationships sooner. They kick themselves for being so blind to get into such relationships with terror lovers in the first place. When the frustrated emotions are uncontrollable, there is a real possibility that something big and bad may happen in the end!"

能又被引發。人最大的焦慮來自於不信任，這個男生真正不信任的其實是自己，也許他這麼做，就是在逃離自己，逃離過去重大的創傷事件，真實的情緒還被壓抑在意識深處……」

「那怎麼辦呢？」小樹很入戲，居然幫這個男生著急起來。

「我已經跟他再約時間，會用回溯與創傷療法探索他的焦慮，進一步幫他。還好，他應該不會再想找你麻煩了。」表姊嘆口氣，「很多年輕人對於分手的挫折無法接受，就直覺地用破壞的方式洩憤，威脅對方，殊不知那只會讓昔日愛人躲得更遠，更不會後悔——只怪沒及早——分手，而是後悔當初怎麼會眼瞎交了恐怖情人。當受挫的情緒無法控制時，最後真的有可能會出大事的！」

"It's easy to fall in love but difficult to break up. Nowadays when young people talk about breaking up, in the end, it is often hurting others and hurting themselves!" Xiaoshu seemed to disagree. Cousin Anli smiled and said, "The reason why emotional wounds are difficult to heal is that when you are rejected by the other party, the emotions of loss will violently impact your mind, causing your body to be highly stressed and your sympathetic nervous system to be hyper excited, which induces anxiety, anger, and other reactions. They are psychologically difficult to adjust in a short time; they need time to heal," cousin Anli said. Then she changed her tone: "Your phone call saved me when I was injured, but I also happened to help you avert a disaster."

"Thank you so much, cousin. It's quite a coincidence. Thanks to you, I was able to avert a potential unwarranted disaster. I told Wang Xiaofang to make an appointment with you for counselling, but I didn't expect things to take such a sudden and dramatic turn for the better."

"You saved me and I helped you, so we are even," Anli laughed and teased.

「這就是相愛容易分手難啦，現在常見年輕人談分手，最後往往就是傷人傷己！」小樹很不以為然。表姊笑著說：「情傷難以化解的原因是，當你被對方拒絕時，失落的情緒會劇烈衝擊內心，讓身體的壓力指數上升，導致交感神經過度亢奮，誘發焦慮、憤怒等反應，心理上是很難在短時間內調適的，這需要時間去撫平！」表姊口氣一轉：「這次無意中，你的一通電話救了我，但我也碰巧讓你避掉一場無妄之災喔！」

　　「太感恩你了，表姊。沒想到這麼巧，幸虧有你才能化解掉可能發生在我身上的無妄之災！我原本還跟王小芳說，要跟你約見面輔導的，沒想到才一下子事情就有了戲劇性轉變。」

　　「你救了我，我也幫了你，我們姊弟倆互不相欠啦！」表姊笑嘻嘻地調侃。

Life is sometimes magical. Something now may presage something else in the future. Perhaps the desire to help others has shone a light in Xiaoshu's heart, which is a light that comes from his good and pure mind that will drive away the darkness hidden around us.

人生有時候就是這麼神奇，沒想到眼前所做的事，會為將來留下伏筆。或許因著想要助人的心念，讓小樹心中燦亮著一道光；而那道源自心善純良的光，必將驅走周遭隱藏的黑黯。

The Magic of A Positive Attitude

If you don't change your negative thinking, your future will become black and white!
Instead of desperately trying to forget the bad memories, it is better to remake good memories for yourself.
Just taking your mind back to the present can alleviate restlessness and suffering.
If you feel like you're not good enough, it means you still have hope in your heart.
Make your heart stronger, and time will patch up your emotional black hole.

正能量的磁場效應

一直不改變負面思考，未來會變成一片黑白！
與其拚命想忘掉不好記憶，不如重編好的記憶給自己
只要讓思緒回到當下，就能減輕不安和痛苦
如果你覺得自己不夠好，代表心中還抱著希望
讓內心覺得更強大，時間會修復情緒黑洞

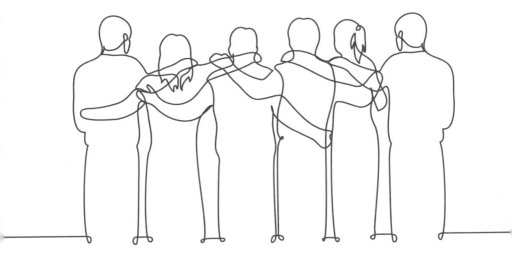

逆境是人生試金石

Adversity is a touchstone of life

Saturday afternoons are the "me time" for Xiaoshu, time for him to get recharged, reenergized. He likes to fill that time to the fullest, ideally with few or no slots unspoken for. That arrangement serves to bottle up the reminiscences of his time with Magician Abo, to be put away at the bottom of his consciousness and gradually forgotten.

On this day, once Xiaoshu had planned his itinerary, he set off on his bicycle. After parking the bike, he sauntered toward his destination, the library. From a distance, the library looked like an aged wooden boat, and from a certain angle, it resembled a large stilted tree house, elevated above the ground. Xiaoshu stepped forward, feeling he was about to enter a treasure trove of knowledge.

Once in the library, the large floor-to-ceiling windows let in the sunlight while presenting visitors with a vantage point from which to take in the neighboring heritage museum, lush trees, small bridges, flowing streams, and landscaping outside the library. The view not just broadens visitors' sight but also relaxes their minds.

Walking in the neatly arranged forest of books, Xiaoshu felt that he was as calm and quiet as a cheetah in the jungle, except his prey, instead of running away from him, was comfortably

每個星期六下午，都是小樹規劃好的充電時間。他想把自己的時間安排得充實飽滿，最好是滴水不漏沒有空檔，這樣就可以把對魔法阿伯的思念，藏進忙碌生活，回歸身體的覺知覺察。

　　今天，小樹計畫好行程就騎上腳踏車出發，停好車後緩步往目的地圖書館走去。遠遠望去，圖書館外觀就像一艘古色古香的木船，從某個角度看，又像是大型的高架樹屋，小樹邁步向前，有種準備入寶山探險尋寶的儀式感。

　　進到圖書館，一片片的大落地窗讓陽光輕快肆意地灑進來，非常巧妙地將館外周遭的古蹟博物館、環抱的蒼鬱大樹、小橋流水與造景框入眼底融為一體，不僅令人視野開闊，也讓人心情放鬆。

　　走在擺放整齊的書林中，小樹覺得自己像叢林獵豹般沉穩安靜而腳步輕盈，只是他的獵物們不會逃跑，而

coming into sight and cheerfully welcoming his visit.

At that moment, he saw his youngest uncle, Rongxi.

Rongxi, ten years older than Xiaoshu, has basically grown up with Xiaoshu. The mature, sensible and gentle uncle has never looked down on Xiaoshu. Instead, he loves and cares for Xiaoshu like his own kid brother. Xiaoshu likewise has regarded the uncle as a big brother, not an elder, not an uncle. Rongxi has never seemed bothered by their way of interaction.

Rongxi started working after graduating from school, and the two of them have not heard from each other since.

Xiaoshu thought about saying hello to his uncle, but noticed that his uncle was frowning and deep in thought. Xiaoshu felt that a dense fog had enveloped Uncle Rongxi so tightly that he couldn't exhale the troubling thoughts in him out of his body. He seemed dizzy and uncomfortable. Was Rongxi trapped by some thorny trouble?

Xiaoshu quickly approached Rongxi.

"Hi, Uncle. It's been a long time."

Startled, Rongxi raised his head and said, "Ah, Xiaoshu. Long time no see. Are you here to read some books, too?"

正以自在的姿態躍入視線範圍，欣喜地歡迎他的探訪。

就在這個時刻，小舅容熙的身影突然映入眼簾。

小舅年長小樹十歲，可說是看著小樹長大。成熟懂事也很溫柔的小舅，從不以長輩自居，也不會倚老賣老，而是像個哥哥般疼愛呵護著小樹。每次跟他說話，小樹往往一不小心就沒大沒小，好像跟自己同學講話一般，而小舅也從不生氣。

小舅從學校畢業到進入職場後，差不多有兩年左右沒跟小樹聯絡了。

小樹剛想過去跟小舅輕聲打個招呼，卻看到他眉頭深鎖，顯露若有所思的神色。小樹關心地看著，感應到小舅四周好像被一團迷霧包裹住，還有股說不出的悶氣在胸中流竄，因為找不到出口而十分難受，感覺他應該是頭昏腦脹很不舒服，難道是被什麼無法解決的煩惱困住了嗎？

小樹快步走到容熙身旁，輕聲打招呼。

「小舅，好久不見。」

被打斷思緒的容熙嚇了一跳，匆忙抬頭小聲回應：

「喔，是小樹啊，好久不見了，你也來看書？」

"Sure. Though ebooks are so prevalent and quite easy to get to, I still like the feeling of flipping the paper pages," Xiaoshu replied.

"Same here. The scent of books and the satisfaction of touch are something that ebooks can never deliver," Rongxi said, delighted to have met people who appreciate physical books. "I'm old school, you know," he continued.

"Me, too."

The two of them smiled knowingly.

Checking his watch, Rongxi said, "I've found the books I want. We don't get to see each other every day. Let me treat you to afternoon tea."

"Sure. I've got my books, too. Let's go. I really want to catch up with you," Xiaoshu replied.

They found a cafe near the library.

Looking happily at the colorful fruit tea in front of him, Xiaoshu said, "I don't like bitter stuff, so I can't drink black coffee. Sweet fruit tea is more to my taste."

Rongxi, sitting opposite, looked a little lost. Staring at his iced coffee, Rongxi smiled wryly and said, "Life sometimes tastes quite bitter, so you might understand why some people like their coffee black after you've grown up."

「對啊，雖然用電子產品讀書直捷又方便，但我還是喜歡翻閱紙本書時的觸感。」小樹輕笑回答。

「我也有這種感覺。書本的氣味跟碰觸時的實在感，這種溫度是電子書永遠無法取代的。」容熙有種找到知音的喜悅，忍不住笑說：「我是老人家。」

小樹也小小聲回應：「我也有個老靈魂。」

兩人很有默契地笑了起來。

容熙看看手錶，建議：「我要借的書已經找好了，難得有機會遇見你，等下小舅請你喝下午茶！」

小樹點點頭，一口答應，「我想借的書也找好了，一起走吧，我也想跟小舅好好聊聊。」

兩人在圖書館附近的咖啡店落坐。

小樹看著眼前色彩繽紛的水果茶，十分滿意：「我不太能吃苦，所以喝不了黑咖啡，還是甜甜的水果茶比較適合我。」

對面的容熙，眼神看來有點失焦，只見它對著自己的冰咖啡苦笑：「人生的滋味有時也很苦澀，等你長大了就會懂冰美式的味道。」

Looking at Rongxi's mournful eyes and listening to his philosophical thoughts, Xiaoshu was quite certain that something was bothering his uncle deep down, not to be revealed. Xiaoshu made up his mind to help his uncle, who wouldn't easily confide to others, resolve whatever it was that's aching him inside.

"Uncle, you checked out a few books about animals. Are they related to what you studied in college, veterinary science?"

"Yes! "A Book of Animal Living and Death", "Animal Hospital No. 39", "One Day in the Life of A Veterinarian", and "The Animal Hospital That Is Super Busy" are all very good books. I want to read these good books again and look back at my initial motivation to study veterinary medicine in the first place. Furthermore, I also want to find my original intention of working for an animal hospital to become a veterinarian."

Xiaoshu smiled and said, "I remember that you also checked out a book called "Don't Fight with Pigs "just now. Is it about a pig farmer or a veterinarian? That title is quite catchy."

A little uneasy, Rongxi hurriedly shook his head to explain, "No, the book is about the philosophy of the workplace and work."

看著小舅，聽他意味深長的話語。小樹很確定小舅藏著心事不想說，於是打定主意要幫不輕易跟人訴苦的小舅打開心結。

　　「小舅，我剛剛看你借了好幾本跟動物有關的書，跟你學獸醫有關嗎？」

　　「是啊！《動物生死書》、《動物醫院 39 號》、《跟著動物醫生過一天》、《好忙好忙的動物醫院》都是很不錯的書。我想重溫這些好書，回想當初讀獸醫系的動機，也想找回到動物醫院當獸醫的初衷。」

　　小樹微笑著，想打開容熙的話匣子：「我記得小舅剛才好像還有借一本書，叫《別跟豬打架》，是講養豬戶還是獸醫的故事嗎？書名挺有趣的。」

　　容熙有點不自在，忙著搖頭解釋，「不是啦，那是一本講職場跟工作哲學的書……」

It had just dawned on Xiaoshu as he nodded and said, "No wonder the cover says 'Don't fight with pigs. It will only make you dirty, but make the pigs happy.' But I'm still wondering what kind of people who raise pigs and fight against pigs?"

Rongxi smiled wryly a little and said, "You are still a student, so you may not know the kinds of problems that may come your way in the workplace. There are many, many problems, and sometimes they can't be avoided at all. And when you encounter them, you know that they are tough to resolve. I want to read this book to learn from others' experience in the hope of resolving my own problems."

"Just because I am a student doesn't mean I know nothing about the workplace. To help pay for my schooling, I have become an experienced part-timer. Besides, there is this possibility that the parties directly involved in a problem may not see things clearly while a bystander, like me, easily sees a resolution clearly," Xiaoshu said.

Rongxi sighed after a moment of silence and began to tell Xiaoshu the trouble that he had encountered: "My boss is very ambitious. He demands efficiency in everything and he has no patience. He is very direct, never beating around the bush or sugar coating things. Tact is not his thing, and he uses foul language at every turn. I always felt very bad every time after he dressed me down."

小樹點點頭，恍然大悟的樣子：「難怪封面寫著：千萬別跟豬打架，這只會讓你變髒，卻讓豬樂在其中。我還在好奇：到底是什麼人養豬還會跟豬打架？」

　　容熙一陣子苦笑：「你還是個學生，可能不了解在工作職場上會碰到怎樣的課題，很多很多，有時候根本沒法預防，遇到了才知道很難解決，我看這本書，是想在別人的經驗裡找到自己問題的答案。」

　　小樹很關心地問：「別看我是學生，就覺得我一定不懂職場的事，我也是有打工賺學費的經驗啊。再說，很多時候當局者迷，說不定我這個旁觀者可以意外提供你不錯的建議呢。」

　　容熙沉靜片刻嘆了口氣，開始訴說自己遇上的麻煩：「我老闆是個很有企圖心的人，他樣樣事情都講求效率，個性又急，所以講話很衝，動不動就罵很難聽的話。每次被他罵，我的情緒就會很差。」

"Verbal abuse can bring on a lot of negative energy and can also make people lose motivation," Xiaoshu said, "Bad language hurts a lot. The boss should respect the employees because, after all, everyone is working for the company, so everyone should be working toward the same goal." Xiaoshu said.

But Rongxi said that his boss was not like that at all, and he went on to demonstrate how his boss sweared: "You people are all pea-brained. You just don't use your brain. Is your brain a decoration? Are you pigs?"

"If you want to expand our business and open a chain of clinics, you need to run it like a business. Use your brain, understand?"

"It's a waste of money to keep you guys on the payroll. A bunch of birdbrains! Pigs!"

His uncle's face turned red with rage. Xiaoshu shook his head; he couldn't believe that the boss would be so verbally abusive. He couldn't help but say, "Pigs are social animals. A boss who loves to scold his people is likely to be a very stupid pig himself." After thinking about it, he felt that it was not right, so he hurriedly added: "No, pigs are very clean and smart, and people can't be called stupid pigs. That's a stereotype, and I shouldn't have called your boss a pig. Pigs, I'm sorry."

「語言暴力會帶來很強的負能量，也會讓人失去動力。」小樹點點頭，他完全理解：「難聽的話很傷人，老闆應該尊重員工，畢竟大家都是為公司而合作努力，目標應該是一致的。」小樹說道。

　　但容熙說他的老闆全然不是如此，他接著模仿老闆罵人的樣子：

　　「你們這些員工真是豬隊友，都不會用腦袋想嗎？腦袋是裝飾品嗎？你是豬嗎？」

　　「想要拓展事業、開連鎖診所，就要企業化經營。好好用腦子，懂嗎？」

　　「養你們這些人真是浪費，豬隊友就是豬隊友！真是笨！」

　　眼看小舅講得臉紅脖子粗的，小樹猛搖頭，覺得他的老闆這樣罵人真的很糟糕，忍不住開口：「豬是群居的動物，愛罵別人豬隊友的老闆，自己也很有可能是頭很笨的豬。」想想又覺得不太對，急忙補充：「不對，豬是很愛乾淨又很聰明的，不能罵人是笨豬，這是刻板印象，也很對不起豬！」

Rongxi couldn't help but smile in agreement, "It seems that Xiaoshu is also fit to be a veterinarian. Yes, all life is precious and valuable, and, as such, should be treated with respect."

Rongxi paused to think for a while before continuing, "I can put up with it if my boss just likes to scold and use bad language because I can selectively tune him out to his malicious swearing. But when it comes to the operation of the veterinary hospital, my boss and I have very different ideas, and this difference in fundamental values makes it very painful."

Rongxi continued to mimic his boss, who was spouting nonsense:

"What you should have done is show me how much profit these outpatient and surgical procedures have brought in, but instead you tried to convince me to buy those expensive medical equipment so you can offer new services."

"If you want to make money, you need to cut expenditure, reduce costs, or find ways to increase your revenue. Therefore, you need to think more about what new fees you can charge our customers and collect more money. Once you've found high-spender customers, you must try to keep them coming back for more services. By the same token, once you've recognized low-spender customers, spend just enough time on them to get them out the door. And if a surgery is too

容熙忍不住笑著同意：「看來小樹也很適合當獸醫呢！沒錯，所有的生命都是珍貴而有價值的，都應該好好尊重與對待。」

容熙想了想，繼續說：「如果只是喜歡罵人、講話難聽，這我還能忍受，反正可以選擇性失聰，讓自己聽不進那些惡意罵人的話就好。但對於獸醫院的經營，我和老闆的理念大不相同，這種基本價值觀的差異讓我很痛苦。」

容熙繼續模仿老闆口沫橫飛的樣子：

「你該做的事是告訴我這些門診跟手術增加了多少利潤，而不是來說服我去買那些很貴的醫療器材，說要增加服務內容。」

「要賺錢就要好好節省支出、降低成本，或想辦法增加收入，那就要多想些名目多收點錢。找到對的貴客要長期用心經營，賺不了錢的那些就應付一下就好，太

troublesome or too tricky, just refer them to other veterinary hospitals. Don't waste your time on them."

"Work hard and do a good job. If you perform well, maybe one day I will make you the head of a branch hospital."

"Everything costs money these days, and we are not here to provide free or money-losing services."

Rongxi was getting more agitated as he carried on his description of his boss. Xiaoshu could sense the pent-up anger in his uncle. "Uncle, did you have any serious conflict with your boss?"

Rongxi nodded: "A few days ago, I was serving Mrs. Wu, a big high-spender customer of ours, who had taken her purebred poodle, Baobao, for a regular checkup, when suddenly a middle-aged man in sportswear rushed in, holding a drooling but unconscious dog.

The man said, "Are you a veterinarian? This is my dog Xiaohuang. I took it to the park for a walk. I don't really know what happened, but perhaps it ate something bad. It got excited and restless at first, then I saw drooling, convulsions, and spasms. Then it passed out. I'm worried that it was poisoned. Please, doctor, please save my dog!"

麻煩或沒把握的手術就介紹他們到別間獸醫院，不用浪費時間。」

「好好幹，如果業績不錯，也許有一天我會讓你當我們獸醫院的分院院長！」

「這個年頭什麼東西都需要錢，免費或虧本的項目不是我們該提供的服務。」

眼看小舅再度越講越激動，小樹一面感受到他鬱結胸口的悶氣，一面關心：「小舅，你跟你老闆是發生了什麼嚴重衝突嗎？」

容熙點點頭：「前幾天，我正在招呼獸醫院的大客戶吳太太，幫她養的一隻叫寶貝的名種貴賓狗做定期健康檢查，這時候突然有個穿運動服的中年男子跑了進來，他抱著一隻流著口水、昏迷的狗，急匆匆地說道……」

「請問你是獸醫嗎？這是我家小黃，我帶牠到公園散步，結果不知道是吃錯了什麼東西，牠起先是興奮、不安，接著流口水、抽搐、痙攣，後來竟然昏迷了。我擔心牠是不是中毒了，拜託醫生，求求你救救牠！」

Rongxi looked at Mrs. Wu's poodle, and then at the anxious man in front of him. He felt that he was in a dilemma.

"But I'm in the middle of an examination. It sounds like your dog has ingested some pesticides. If there is no spasm, you can wash it with water as soon as possible, but if there is a spasm, immediate first aid is required. That's right. You've properly handled it. Xiaohuang needs to be treated right away," Rongxi said.

That made Mrs. Wu very unhappy, and she wasted no time protesting: "My baby has made an appointment in advance, and we came in first. How in the world can this gentleman cut the line?"

The man, flustered, said, "Xiaohuang is like my family, and I can't imagine what I would do if I lost it. Please, please, doctor! Please, save my dog!"

Mrs. Wu insisted: "I don't care. I have a tight schedule, and I came here first. You should follow the rules and make an appointment with the doctor. The doctor should check my baby first!" She turned her head to glare at Rongxi and said, "May I remind you that I'm a VIP here, and my baby is a purebred, and this man's dog is apparently a mongrel. Things have priorities, and you should know who has the first priority and what is urgent."

容熙看看吳太太的貴賓狗，再看看眼前這位焦急的男子，有點左右為難。

　　「可是我現在還有一隻狗正在檢查……聽起來，你的狗狗應該是誤食了含有殺蟲劑的東西，如果還沒有出現痙攣，可以趕快用水清洗，若是發生痙攣了就要馬上急救。沒錯，你的處理是對的，小黃需要馬上治療……」

　　一旁的吳太太聽了很不高興，馬上抗議：「我家寶貝事先已經約好時間，我們是先來的，這位先生怎麼可以插隊？」

　　男子表情慌張：「小黃就像我的家人，我真不敢想像萬一失去牠的話，我該怎麼辦？拜託拜託，醫生！拜託你救救小黃！」

　　吳太太很堅持：「不管，我的時間寶貴，是我先來的，你應該照規矩跟醫生再約時間，醫生應該先幫我家寶貝檢查！」她轉頭瞪著容熙：「我是 VIP 喔，我家寶貝是名犬，這位先生養的小黃是不知哪裡來的狗；事有輕重緩急，誰先、誰急，你應該很清楚！」

"Of course I know that there are priorities, and saving a life is absolutely a priority," Rongxi said very firmly. Then he quickly turned around and walked towards Xiaohuang, "I will first give Xiaohuang a blood test to get its blood sugar, liver and kidney function, and assess its poisonous ingestion, and then I'll give it activated carbon and other treatments to reduce the concentration of pesticides in Xiaohuang's body."

Then he turned around and said solemnly, "Mrs. Wu, I'm sorry, but I need to ask you and your baby dog to please wait for me."

Mrs. Wu was incredulous, her facial expression becoming more and more unpleasant. She raised her voice and roared sharply, "What? You want me to wait! Is that mixed dog from nowhere so important? One penny can get you a dozen of that type of dog; yes, that's how cheap they are on the streets. How can you compare it with my baby?" She gritted her teeth and rebuked, "You will definitely regret the decision you made just now. I'll see to it, and I will complain to your boss!"

Xiaoshu, taking a deep breath, said, "I just know that uncle would definitely save Xiaohuang first, but what happened next?"

「我當然知道事有輕重緩急，搶時間救命絕對要優先！」容熙很篤定地說。然後迅速轉身走向小黃，「我先幫中毒的小黃進行血液檢驗，確認血糖、肝腎功能跟誤食狀況，再給予活性碳等治療，降低小黃體內的藥劑濃度。」

接著轉身滿懷歉意地鄭重跟吳太太說：「吳太太，對不起，要麻煩你跟你家寶貝等我一下。」

吳太太一臉不敢置信，神情愈來愈難看，提高聲量尖利咆嘯：「什麼？！居然要我等！那隻不知從哪來的狗有這麼重要嗎？外面滿街跑，要多少有多少，怎能跟我家寶貝比？」她怒氣沖沖、咬牙切齒地斥責：「你一定會後悔你現在做的決定，我要向你老闆投訴！」

聽聞容熙陳述事情經過，小樹深吸一口氣：「我知道小舅肯定會先救小黃，那後來呢？」

Rongxi smiled wryly and said, "Xiaohuang is saved. I was moved to see its owner cry when it slowly wagged its tail after it had regained consciousness. I was also touched by the sense of accomplishment and the joy of saving a life!"

Sighing, Rongxi continued, "Mrs. Wu believed that she had been delayed, so she was very angry. Sure enough, my boss dressed me down. Just for this incident, he scolded and otherwise verbally abused me more than ten times! He also said that he would withhold half of my monthly salary." Rongxi frowned and shook his head, "He chewed me up for mindlessly offending a VIP customer and her prestigious purebred dog for the sake of saving a cheap dog whose owner wore nothing more than cheap sportswear." Rongxi's eyes showed his anger as he continued, "He just could not stop scolding me and saying that a small, brainless vet like me who can't tell what's really important is not qualified to head a branch hospital at all!" Rongxi was almost crying by now, but he continued, "I can't forget his expression, looking at me with real disdain and simply looking down on me!"

"It's tough to work for a person with different values. Very hard to get your points across," Xiaoshu said. His uncle looked happy at one moment, angry the next, and lost after

容熙苦笑著説：「小黃得救了。看到牠恢復精神後緩緩搖著尾巴，牠的主人感動地掉下淚來，我也很感動，那種拯救了一個生命的成就感與快樂是無價的！」

　　嘆了口氣，容熙接著無奈地補充：「不過，吳太太認為被耽誤了時間，所以非常生氣，我也被老闆罵慘了！光為這件事，他罵我是不長腦的豬隊友，罵了不只十次！還説要扣我半個月的薪水！」容熙皺著眉搖頭：「他大罵我，竟然會為了穿廉價運動服、養混種狗的陌生客人，大膽冒犯、得罪了名犬主人 VIP 客戶！」一時之間，容熙眼神露出了憤怒：「他還一直碎念罵説，這種分不清楚事情輕重緩急的小醫生，根本沒資格當獸醫院分院院長！」講到這，容熙兩眼通紅：「我始終忘不了他的表情，真的很不屑、很看不起人的樣子！」

　　「跟價值觀不同的人共事真是辛苦，太難溝通了！」小樹看著臉上陰晴不定，一下開心、一下氣憤、

that, seemingly to experience shifting emotions. Xiaoshu couldn't help but ask curiously, "Uncle, suppose heading a branch hospital is your goal, do you regret your action to save Xiaohuang while going against the will of the boss and offending a VIP customer?"

Rongxi thought for a moment and said firmly, "No, I don't regret it at all. If it were to happen all over again, I would still do it again!" Right at that moment, Rongxi's eyes lit up, and his tone was resolute, "Life is priceless. That is why I chose to become a veterinarian in the first place. My original intention is to love animals and protect life!"

It's strange to say, at this moment, Xiaoshu sensed a brilliant light projected on his uncle, causing the fog around him to quickly dissipate, and the sluggish qi flowing in his chest disappeared. Unconsciously, the uncle said that his head was no longer swollen and painful.

It might seem strange, but at this moment, Xiaoshu sensed a brilliant light had just dawned on his uncle because the anger, anguish, and pain in Rongxi had quickly dissipated. Rongxi said that his head was no longer swollen and aching.

一下又失落的小舅，忍不住好奇地問：「小舅，假設擔任獸醫院分院院長是你的努力目標，那你違背老闆的意思先搶救小黃，以致得罪 VIP 客戶，你會感到後悔嗎？」

容熙思索了一下，堅定地說：「不，我想就算事情重來一次，我還是會這麼做！」說到這，容熙眼睛亮起來了，語氣堅決：「生命是無價的，這也是我當初選擇當獸醫的原因。我的初衷就是要愛護動物、守護生命！」

說也奇怪，這一刻小樹感應到有股燦爛的光投射在小舅身上，讓他四周的迷霧迅速散去，胸口流竄的鬱結之氣也消失了。不覺間，小舅說他的頭不再脹痛了。

Looking at Rongxi's clear eyes, Xiaoshu smiled knowingly and said softly, "Uncle, I think you should think about it and decide what to do next!"

Rongxi nodded: "Xiaoshu, you are really amazing. I've just talked to you briefly, but I think I've been able to put the whole thing in order and in proper perspective. I've sorted it out."

Xiaoshu smiled and waited for Rongxi's conclusion.

"After this incident and my boss's violent reaction, I have a crystal clear picture of my innermost values. I know what kind of vet I want to be, and I know what kind of boss I don't want to be! I don't want to be the head of a very profitable branch veterinary hospital at all. What I really want is to be a good veterinarian who loves animals and protects life!"

Xiaoshu nodded and happily pointed to the photo of himself and his dog Laifu on his mobile phone and said, "If there is anything wrong with Laifu, I will definitely seek you out for help. You're the best vet in my heart."

Rongxi handed out his business card to Xiaoshu and said, "Even if I quit working for this veterinary hospital, you can still call me on my cell phone. If there is anything that Laifu needs, I will do my best."

看著小舅清透的眼神，小樹露出會心微笑，輕輕地說：「小舅，我覺得你應該想好也決定好接下來該怎麼做了！」

　　容熙點點頭：「小樹真是厲害！才跟你聊一下，我覺得已經能把整件事整理一遍，我已經想清楚了！」

　　小樹微笑著等待容熙說出結論。

　　「經過這次事件跟我老闆的暴怒反應，我清楚確認內心深處的價值觀。我知道我想成為哪一種獸醫，也明白我不想成為哪一種老闆！我根本不想當個很會賺錢的獸醫院分院院長，我真正想要的是做個愛護動物、守護生命的好獸醫！」

　　小樹點點頭，開心地指著手機裡自己跟愛犬來福的合照說：「如果我家的來福有哪裡不舒服，我一定會帶牠來找你。你是我心目中最棒的好獸醫！」

　　容熙遞出自己的名片給小樹，很高興地指著上面的號碼：「就算哪一天我不在這間獸醫院工作了，你還是可以打手機找我。來福有需要我幫忙的地方，我一定全力以赴。」

After a moment of silence, Xiaoshu looked at Rongxi very seriously and said to Rongxi, "Gold always shines, so no matter what you decide to do, I will always cheer for you!"

Rongxi nodded and patted Xiaoshu on the shoulder: "Thank you, Xiaoshu. Being a bystander, you helped me look at my affairs from another perspective, and I have objectively found the answer to my question."

"I hope that the next time we meet, I can hear an update to your new situation and good news. I wish you the best," Xiaoshu said.

The two of them high-fived knowingly and said goodbye.

Three weeks later, Xiaoshu went to the library to return the books and met Rongxi again. This time, Rongxi was not only clear-headed but also more confident.

Walking outside the library with his uncle, Xiaoshu couldn't wait to say, "Thank you for curing the stray cat that my classmate had picked up."

"Your classmate is very loving. That poor stray cat was bitten by a stray dog, and its wound just kept bleeding. Fortunately, your classmate had brought the cat in timely, otherwise its right leg would have been lame."

小樹沉默了一下，很認真地看著容熙：「是金子總會發光，不論小舅決定怎麼做，我會一直為你加油！」

　　容熙點點頭，拍拍小樹的肩膀：「謝謝你這個旁觀者，讓我換個角度，客觀地找到問題的答案！」

　　「希望下次見面時，能聽到小舅的新狀況與好消息，祝福你！」舅甥兩人默契地開心擊掌作別。

　　三週後，小樹到圖書館準備還書，意外再度與小舅相遇。這次感應到他不但神清氣爽也更有自信，身上不時投射出溫暖的熱度與光芒。

　　陪著小舅在圖書館外散步，小樹迫不及待地開口：「上次幸虧有小舅幫忙，治好了我同學撿到的流浪貓。」

　　「你同學很有愛心，可憐的流浪貓被流浪狗咬傷後，傷口一直流血不止；還好你同學及時把貓咪送來，不然牠右腳就瘸了！」

Xiaoshu couldn't thank Rongxi enough: "My classmate admires you very much. He said that you are an excellent vet and a wonderful person, and you didn't charge him anything."

Rongxii said, "He said that you're his classmate, and he was helping a stray cat, so I used my salary to pay for his visit."

"Ah, you paid for it," Xiaoshu said. Rongxi smiled and said, "It's nothing. That cat was the last case I did at that hospital anyway."

Xiaoshu said, "Uncle, are you quitting? Which veterinary hospital do you plan to work for next?"

Rongxi said slowly, "After curing your classmate's stray cat, I submitted my resignation to the boss."

"It was an amicable split with your boss, right?"

"Yes, we parted ways without hard feelings. Seriously, in fact, I am still very grateful to the boss, who gave me the opportunity to be a veterinarian in the first place. I wish him the best to find the right person as the head of the veterinary hospital branch that meets his ideals. Finally, I gently reminded him that if he would praise others somewhat, he would give people encouragement and build their confidence, and he would be more popular."

小樹很感謝容熙：「我同學好崇拜你，他説你醫術高明，人又好，還不收他的錢。」

　　容熙真誠地説：「他説是你同學，又是幫忙流浪貓，我就用我的薪水私下幫他抵了醫療費用啦。」

　　「啊！讓小舅破費了！」原來是小舅買單，小樹更感恩了。容熙笑説：「沒關係，反正那是我在那間獸醫院最後一個案子了，就讓老闆扣錢吧。」

　　好爽快的小舅舅，小樹關心地問：「小舅你要離職啦？準備要換去哪間獸醫院？」

　　容熙緩緩説道：「治好了你同學的流浪貓之後，我就跟老闆辭職了！」

　　「你該不是跟老闆鬧得不歡而散、吵架負氣才離開的吧？」

　　「沒有喔，我是在很平和的氣氛下離職的。説真的，其實我還是很感謝老闆，當初是他讓我有機會當獸醫，祝福他能找到符合心目中理想的獸醫院分院院長。最後我還婉轉提醒他：懂得適度稱讚別人，讓人得到鼓勵與建立信心，人氣會更旺喔。」

Xiaoshu nodded: "I have already guessed as much. Uncle is a good person, so you will not talk in hurtful language."

"After all, I also hope that the my replacement veterinarian will no longer have to endure the pain and torture I have suffered, and I also hope that the boss will respect life more and understand that money and performance are really not the most important things."

Xiaoshu admired Rongxi's largehearteness. Then he said something that he had heard before, though not remembering where, "Sometimes adversity makes people more and more courageous, and when they calm down, they can also see clearly what is truly valuable."

"Yes, when I worked at that veterinary hospital, I was always unhappy, but I always thought that I would just tough it out. It wasn't until after the Xiaohuang incident that I finally came to my senses—thanks to the unceasing scolding from the boss." Rongxi looked at Xiaoshu and said sincerely, "And your words also helped me make up my mind."

"What did I say? I talked a lot that day," Xiaoshu said.

小樹點點頭：「這個我早就猜到了，小舅是個好人，就算離職也不會口出惡言的。」

　　「畢竟我也希望接替我工作的下一個獸醫，不用再忍受我曾經受到的痛苦與折磨，也希望老闆能多尊重每一個生命，理解到錢跟業績真的不是最重要的！」

　　小樹很佩服容熙的氣度，想到不知從哪聽來的話與小舅分享：「有時候人在逆境的時候會愈挫愈勇，冷靜下來也可以看清楚真正的價值到底是什麼。」

　　「是呀，我在那家獸醫院工作的時候，一直很不開心，可是總想著辛苦點沒關係，忍忍就過去了。直到那次小黃事件後，我才真正被老闆罵醒！」容熙看著小樹真誠的說：「還有你的話也讓我下定決心。」

　　「哪句話？我說了好多話呢。」小樹有點疑惑。

"It's hard to work with people who have different values!" Rongxi emphasized, "And you asked me, 'Uncle, suppose heading a branch hospital is your goal, do you regret your action to save Xiaohuang while going against the will of the boss...?' It helped me re-examine my own values and clarify what I really wanted."

"I didn't know that I was so smart," Xiaoshu was a little proud of himself when he heard this. Then Rongxi said playfully, "But there is one thing that even you would not be able to guess."

Curiosity piqued, Xiaoshu said, "What is it? Uncle, just tell me."

"I was surprised to find out who that middle-aged man who came with the poisoned dog was. It turned out that he is a very well-known Facebook community moderator Huang Douge. His community has attracted thousands of followers. The purpose of the community is to love animals and respect life. Everyone likes to share the tidbits about their pets on it. Many people don't keep famous breeds of cats and dogs, but instead they keep stray animals. The members and fans of that community are all very loving, and they will exchange information with each other."

「跟價值觀不同的人共事真是辛苦！」容熙強調，「還有你問我，如果擔任獸醫院分院院長是我的目標，但我卻跟老闆唱反調，這事我會後悔嗎？這讓我重新面對自己內心，認清我真正想要的是什麼。」

　　「原來我很高明喔！」小樹聞言有點得意，卻見容熙眨眨眼俏皮地說：「可是有一件事，聰明的你應該也猜不到！」

　　小樹忍不住好奇地問：「什麼事？小舅，你就別賣關子了，快說！快說！」

　　「我也沒想到，那個抱著中毒的狗來急救的中年男子，竟然是非常有名的臉書社團版主黃豆格，那個社團有好幾千人追蹤呢，社團宗旨是愛護動物、尊重生命，大家喜歡在上面分享自己養寵物的點點滴滴，很多人養的都不是名種貓犬，而是街上撿來的流浪動物，所以不論社員或粉絲都很有愛心，也會互相交流相關資訊。」

"Wow! Uncle is not becoming an Internet celebrity because of this, is he? Therefore, don't judge people by their appearance. No, rather, don't judge dogs by their appearance." Xiaoshu said with a smile.

"You guessed it! In words and in photos, Huang Douge vividly and emotionally shared the story and process of my treatment of Xiaohuang, which close to ten thousand people liked and close to 3,000 shared," Rongxi said.

"Wow! That's amazing. That's just great. My uncle has become an Internet celebrity. I want to tell my classmates so everyone can like and share."

Rongxi, smiling a little shyly, said, "Being famous really wasn't my original goal. You know I was just anxious to save Xiaohuang's life at that time, and I didn't think about other things."

Xiaoshu nodded and smiled in agreement: "I understand. Uncle, you are a good veterinarian, and fame and fortune are not your goal."

"As soon as Huang Douge heard that I was leaving the veterinary hospital where he and I first met, he immediately announced it to the community, asking everyone to submit information about a good veterinary hospital that was looking for a good partner."

「嘎！小舅該不會因此成了網路名人吧？！所以說人不可貌相，絕對不要以貌取人！不是啦，是不要以貌取狗。」小樹笑笑說著。

「你猜對啦！黃豆格把我治療小黃的過程以文字加照片的方式，生動感性地分享出來，結果社群有上萬人按讚，還有近三千人分享。」

「哇！那可不得了，太讚了，我的小舅變成網紅了！我要跟同學講，讓大家都去按讚分享！」

容熙笑得有點靦腆：「出名真的不是我當初的目的，那時候我只是一心急著要救小黃的命，沒想那麼多。」

小樹點頭微笑認同：「我懂，小舅是個好獸醫，名利並不是你的目標。」

「黃豆格一聽說我要離開原來的獸醫院，馬上熱心地幫我在社團宣傳，問大家有沒有認識正在找好夥伴的優良獸醫院。」

"Wow. This would be much faster and more effective than going to HR websites to post information, wait for notifications, and then arrange an interview for a job."

"That's right, word quickly spread through technology and networks, and I immediately received several job offers. Some people even proposed that, if I wanted to open a veterinary clinic, I could consider collaborations in which I would contribute manpower and technology and they would furnish the funds. That was completely beyond my wildest dreams."

Amazed, Xiaoshu said, "At first I thought you were a benefactor of Xiaohuang and Huang Douge, but Huang Douge turns out to be your benefactor who has helped you connect with so many possibilities."

Rongxi thought for a while and said with a smile, "I have many benefactors: Huang Douge has helped me a lot, led me to several good job prospects, and shown me that there are a lot of caring people. So, yes, Huang Douge is my benefactor, but Xiaoshu, you are also my benefactor: you listened to my troubles, helped me see myself more clearly, and guided me to sort out my confusion."

「哇！這可是比上人力網站辛苦登錄資料、等候通知、再安排面試去應徵工作更迅速有效！」

　　「沒錯，透過科技與人脈廣宣效益，我馬上就有好幾個工作可以選，還有人主動跟我説，如果我有意願開獸醫診所，可以考慮合作，我出人力跟技術、他們投資，這根本是我之前完全想不到的！」

　　小樹睜大眼睛讚嘆：「哇！我以為小舅是小黃跟黃豆格的貴人，原來黃豆格才真的是你的貴人，幫你牽了很多好緣呢！」

　　容熙思索了一會兒，輕輕笑了笑，「我的貴人很多，黃豆格是一個，他幫了我好多，介紹了好幾個不錯的工作，也讓我認識了很多有愛心的人；小樹你又何嘗不是我的貴人呢，你傾聽我的煩惱，從旁協助我重新看清楚自己，也幫我解決了困惑。」

Then a lightbulb went on in Xiaoshu just before he said, "Speaking of who is helping whom, your former boss who liked to unceasingly torment you with abusive language and that not-give-an-inch VIP Mrs. Wu can both be regarded as your benefactors. You see, some benefactors lead the way for you, while other benefactors force you to work extra hard in order to get away from a dead-end job that you dreaded. Sometimes, adversity brings out your inner strength and makes you shine."

Rongxi was thoroughly delighted and enlightened. He said, "You are right on. Our benefactors are all around us. Okay, now please allow me the pleasure of taking you, my little benefactor, to afternoon tea, but this time, I will try the fruit tea that you ordered the last time. Sweet, bitter, and sour are all good parts of life."

"Then I will try the bitter iced black coffee that you ordered the last time. In life, you have to have the courage to try!"

小樹福至心靈地説：「這麼説起來，喜歡罵人的前老闆跟很凶的 VIP 吳太太，也算是你的貴人喔！有的貴人會為你帶路，有的貴人會刺激你、促使你努力找到正確的路，所以他們也都是你的貴人呢！有時候通過逆境的考驗，更有機會讓自己發光發熱！」

　　容熙打從心裡服氣，肯定地説：「沒錯，周圍都是我們的貴人！好，讓我請小貴人去吃下午茶，這次，我想試試你上回點的水果茶！人生，有苦有回甘，也有酸酸甜甜的好味道！」

　　「那換我試試冰美式，挑戰一下苦後的回甘。人生，要勇於嘗試！」

The Magic of A Positive Attitude

When fear and worry cloud your eyes
Others can't see your true self
And you can't see their sincerity
The criterion of choice should not be fear, but love
Choose not out of fear or a desire to shun
Choose out of love as it open our hearts

正能量的磁場效應

當恐懼和擔心遮蔽了雙眼

別人看不到自己真實的一面

自己也看不到對方真誠的樣貌

選擇的標準不應該是恐懼，而是愛

不是因為害怕或為了逃避而選擇

以愛為基準做的選擇，可以讓我們的心更開闊

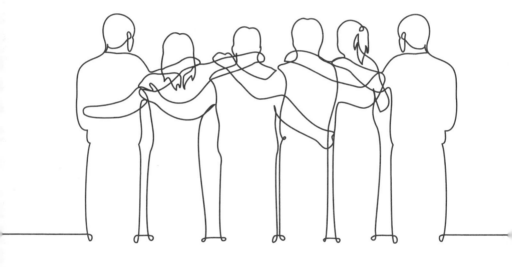

第三章
CHAPTER 3

失落的哀傷情緒

Loss and grief

With the sun bright and the breeze gentle, it's going to be a really nice day. Something good is bound to happen today.

After cheerfully finishing what he needed to do at the bookstore, Xiaoshu walked down the street. Approaching a bakery, he felt a sudden and great hunger—no doubt aroused by the aroma of baking. He wanted to go inside to buy something to eat, but he didn't really want to contend with waiting in the long line at the cash registers. As he hesitated at the store front, someone pushed him from behind. Xiaoshu turned and saw a man in a cap with his head lowered. Without uttering an apology, the man turned around and left hurriedly. Xiaoshu paid the incident no heed at the moment. Instead he followed the crowd into the bakery. When he was ready to check out, he got in the queue and found that his wallet was missing. He suspected that the man who had bumped into him outside the bakery just now was a pickpocket. Xiaoshu put down the bread and rushed out the door to find that man, but of course that man was nowhere to be seen.

"Rats! Why me? What's wrong with him, taking the few dollars I had left for some bread? What a lowlife! Why did he have to make me go home hungry?" Standing at the

陽光普照，微風習習，真是好天氣，一定會有好事發生！

小樹愉快地逛完書局後，優閒漫步在街上，經過一家麵包店時，一陣香味撲鼻而來，他突然感覺肚子餓了，就想進去買麵包果腹，但看到滿滿的人潮，有點懶得排隊，正站在門口猶豫間，突然有人從後面推了他一把，小樹轉頭看，那人戴著鴨舌帽，頭低低的也沒說道歉，就匆忙地轉身迅速離開。小樹當下也不以為意，跟著人潮擠進店內挑選麵包，但就在他一邊排隊一邊掏著腰包準備結帳時，才發現錢包竟不翼而飛了！他回想莫非剛才推他一把的人是扒手？小樹趕緊放下麵包，奪門而出要找尋那戴鴨舌帽的人，但四處張望總沒看到嫌疑犯的蹤影！

「怎麼這樣，我跟他有仇嗎？連我身上僅剩買麵包的錢也要偷，真欺負人啊！真是太惡劣了，這是要叫我

intersection and seeing nobody around, the more Xiaoshu thought about it, the angrier he became, so much so that he slammed a telephone pole. Suddenly an old man next to him said, "Young man, the telephone pole didn't offend you, did it? It's useless to be angry. Think about the bright side, and good things will happen." Without saying another word, the old man crossed the street and disappeared.

"How can I come up with a silver lining when I just had such rotten luck? Don't tell me that I should feel happy for the thief." Unable to quiet himself from the sense of loss, Xiaoshu idly stood at the intersection. After he had calmed down a little, he remembered the game of "seeing the bright side in everything in life" he played with team leader Wu a while back. It's a simple game: a group of people sit in a circle, surrounding a moderator. The moderator proposes a topic for everyone to ponder on–provided that they "see the bright side in everything in life"–and then everyone shares their thoughts in an ensuing discussion.

The game serves to remind a person that if one practices the game diligently and thinks about the bright side in everything along their path, their mood brightens up measurably.

餓肚子回家嗎？」站在路口四顧無人，小樹愈想愈氣，憤怒地捶了一下電線桿，突然旁邊一位老人開口了：

「年輕人，電線桿沒有得罪你吧？生氣無益，凡事往好處想，才會有好事發生喔。」說完，就老人就逕自過馬路了。

「遇到這麼倒霉的事，要如何往好處想？總不能想，偷我錢的人此刻一定很高興吧！」一時還無法扭轉失落情緒，小樹在路口呆立了一會兒，待激動的心情稍微冷靜下來，他想起上次跟吳小隊長他們玩的「凡事往好處想」的遊戲。遊戲很簡單：一群人圍坐成圈，主持人在中央，由他提出一個題目，大家就各自思索細想——前提是一定要「凡事往好處想」——然後再分享各自的看法，透過彼此討論，交流心情和想法。

遊戲的目的是要提醒我們：

要時刻勤加練習，凡事往好處想，整個心情就會變得不一樣。

The thought of the game immediately comforted Xiaoshu, and he told himself: "Fortunately, it is only a beat-up billfold with a mere NT$300 in it, and my ID cards and student fare card can be replaced easily enough."

Magically, this thought seemed to have injected vigor into him, who just moments before had been downbeat and listless from the loss of a billfold. He cheered up as he made his way toward a police station to report the theft. As he walked, he saw broken glass bottles in an alleyway. He was going to just kick them to the side of the road so that people would not get hurt, but then he thought that it would be safer to wrap the shards in paper towels and throw them away. He bent down to pick up the pieces, which gave off the smell of stale alcohol. As he touched the shards, he faintly heard someone sobbing, but a careful inspection of his surroundings yielded no evidence of a person.

Now he turned his attention to finding a recycling bin and trash can. When he finally came across one, he approached it. As he was about to throw in the shards, he saw something familiar. It was his lost billfold, which had made its way back to its rightful owner. Xiaoshu was elated. As expected, the NT$300 was gone, but the other stuff was intact, sparing him

想到這，小樹適時地勸慰自己：「還好那是個舊錢包，而且裡面只有三百元，身分證與學生車票也還可以重新申請補辦。」

　　原本無精打采的他，往好處想後就打起了精神，準備要先去警察局報案。走著走著，在小巷街道中他看到有碎玻璃瓶，本想踢到路旁去免得傷人，但想想，還是用紙巾包起來丟掉比較安全。他彎下腰撿拾，聞到碎片有酒味，在碰觸剎那竟隱約聽到有微弱的哭泣聲，小樹仔細地環顧四周，發現並沒有人呀！

　　搜尋無果，他只好先去找路邊的資源回收桶。邊找邊走了好一段路，才終於看到，在丟入玻璃碎片時，小樹眼角餘光掃到垃圾桶旁有東西看著眼熟，細看竟然是他遭竊的錢包，失而復得！哈哈，小樹開心極了，雖然裡頭的三百元肯定沒啦，但幸好身分證、車票都還在。

the trouble of getting replacements. The thief was kind enough to do the least damage, so instead of throwing the billfold into the trash can, he put it beside, perhaps thinking that somebody would find it and send it to the lost and found at a police station. The practice of looking at the bright side seemed to have already worked for Xiaoshu.

When he got home, Xiaoshu recalled the sobbing sound he heard when he picked up the glass shards, and he suddenly had the urge to go through old photos to see if anyone he knew might need help.

He identified nobody after flipping through the album a few times, and Xiaoshu sat for a moment, thinking that maybe he had heard it wrong at the time, so he didn't pursue it further.

Suddenly, the phone rang, and it was Team Leader Wu calling. "Do you want to go to the mountains to visit that family again?" he asked, referring to the family of a man in his 60s who took care of more than 700 stray dogs in the Stray Animal Shelter. All his children suffer from one form of mental disorder or another. "The mountain road is very steep and narrow, and everyone was scared that they might fall off the cliff when they got out of the car. Do you remember them?" The team leader tries to jog Xiaoshu's memory.

凡事往好處想，小樹覺得偷竊者還是有點良心，他本來大可把錢包丟進垃圾桶毀屍滅跡，但他把錢包丟在垃圾桶外面，也是想要讓人發現送去警察局，這樣失主至少不用補辦一堆證件吧？

回到家，小樹再次回想起撿拾玻璃碎片時一度聽到的啜泣聲，他突然有個念頭要去翻舊照片，看看是否有認識的人需要幫忙？

相簿前後翻了幾次，竟絲毫感受不到任何情緒，小樹呆坐片刻，心想也許當時是自己恍神聽錯，就沒有再追究下去。

突然鈴聲響起，是吳小隊長打電話來：「要不要再去山區關懷那家人？六十幾歲的阿伯，在流浪動物關懷協會照顧七百多隻流浪狗，兒女都有精神障礙，你記得嗎？山區道路很陡很小，下車都很怕會掉到崁底，你有印象嗎？」小隊長試圖喚起小樹的記憶。

"His wife, Atao, drinks too much. Once she had too much to drink and got so drunk as to fall down a hill, and she was such a heavyset that even four men could not pull her up. Remember that? Their home is in the mountains, so they often see animals that are rare on the flat land, such as cobras getting in their house in winter trying to get warm. Initially, there were five people in their family, but the eldest son passed away, so now the couple is raising a pair of disabled children. Their daughter also gave birth to a grandson unexpectedly, but she didn't even know who the biological father was!"

After the team leader had mentioned all those anecdotes in one breath, Xiaoshu was finally able to recall the family in question. He now remembered that the man's son would hide under the covers all day long and refuse to go outdoors, and if he went outside, he would throw a fit and smash the cars that happened to be in his path.

"The couple have never given up on their children," the team leader continued, "Because their eldest son passed away, and their other son was once placed in a children's shelter. Atao is worried every day about losing her only son again, so she drinks heavily as a way to divert her fears. It is suspected that she was also suffering from depression, and she cried all

「他老婆叫阿桃，很愛喝酒，曾經還喝醉酒跌落山坡，因為體重過重，出動四個男人都拉不起來，你還記得吧？還有，他們家在山裡，經常會遇到平地少見的動物，像冬天還會有眼鏡蛇進他們屋裡取暖。原本他們家有五口人，後來長子不幸往生，現在夫妻倆撫養著一雙身心障礙的兒女；女兒還意外生了個孫子，卻連生父是誰都不知道！」

小隊長一口氣說出這麼多，終於讓小樹想起來了。對，印象中阿伯的兒子成天都躲在被窩不肯出門，只要出門就心情不好亂砸路邊車子。

「他們這對父母對孩子始終不離不棄，」小隊長接著說：「因為大兒子已不幸往生，現在這小兒子曾經被安置在療養院，阿桃很害怕再度失去僅有的兒子！因為每天都擔心受怕，她因此借酒澆愁，似乎也疑似患了憂

the time!" Hearing this, Xiaoshu thought about the crying he had heard vaguely when he picked up the glass shards.

Xiaoshu believes that Atao must be anxious and at a loss, so he empathizes with Atao from the bottom of his heart.

"I still remember her husband said that he had met Atao through a matchmaker. His mother liked Atao because she believed that Atao's looks boded well for the future prosperity of his family, so, out of his filial duty, he married Atao in accordance with his mother's wishes. After the wedding, he found out that Atao was afflicted with a psychiatric disorder with symptoms that were sometimes more pronounced than others. Despite this, he accepted Atao as his fate, and Atao returned the favor by taking good care of him. This couple have depended on each other as they form a family," said the team leader.

Xiaoshu said, "I remember the first time I went to their house; the house on the hill was crude and cluttered. It smelled bad, even with a stench of urine. We helped them change bedsheets and replaced the lamps. Are they doing all right now?" Xiaoshu wondered how their only living son was doing and believed that he ought to be taken to a psychiatrist for an evaluation on whether he needed to be hospitalized.

鬱症，經常都在哭泣！」聽到這，小樹想起撿拾碎玻璃片時依稀聽聞的哭泣聲。

「她一定很焦慮，不知道該如何排解？」小樹從心底同理阿桃。

「我還記得阿伯說，當初是經人介紹，相親時母親稱讚阿桃長得有福相，孝順的阿伯聽從母意就娶了阿桃。婚後才發現，阿桃是後天的精障，時好時壞，儘管如此，阿伯也是認命和她過日子。生性單純的阿桃，對阿伯也是照顧有加，貧賤夫妻相依為命，就這樣組了一個家庭。」小隊長接著說道。

「我還記得第一次去他們家，山上的房屋很簡陋，屋裡堆滿了各種雜物，很臭，還有尿騷味。我們曾去幫忙換床單和燈管，他們現在生活沒問題吧？」說到這，小樹心中念頭一轉：不知道她兒子現在怎麼樣了？小樹覺得應該帶他去給精神科醫師看看，是否有入院治療的需要？

"So far many people have chipped in enough to cover their living expenses. And volunteers have renovated their house, so snakes can no longer get into the house. Now it's the psychiatric issues that we are worried about. Do you want to go with us?" the team leader asked Xiaoshu.

Xiaoshu consented, so the team leader picked up Xiaoshu and Dr. Chen, a psychiatrist, as they set out. Soon the car started winding its way up the mountains where the road became steeper and narrower as it became a dirt road. The drive was treacherous.

Finally they arrived at the destination, and indeed as the team leader had said, their renovated house, far from crude, looked like a new house. Although most of the household items such as the refrigerator, cabinets, and beds in the house are previously used that others had given them, they also looked quite new because all items had been refurbished.

"Wow! Your house is nice. It's like new. How are you and your family doing, sir?" said the team leader.

"Thanks to the help of volunteers, the improved condition of the house surely feels better. My son is doing much better now, and he even helps care for the dogs at the stray dogs shelter. Thank you very much," the man couldn't thank the visitors enough.

「他們現在得到各方資助，生活上已沒問題，志工也幫他們把房子整修好了，蛇類也進不了屋裡啦。現在要關懷的就是精神方面的問題了，你要一起去嗎？」小隊長為小樹更新資訊並邀他同行。

　　於是，小隊長開車，帶上小樹與精神科陳醫師一起出發，從平地到山間蜿蜒而上，路越走越陡、路面越來越窄，從柏油路到土路山徑，一路可謂驚險萬分。

　　好不容易到達目的地，確實如小隊長所說，阿伯家的房子已經不像從前那麼簡陋，整修得如同新屋一般。雖然屋裡的冰箱、櫃子、床鋪等生活用具多數是捐贈的二手品，但也都經過整理有如新品。

　　「哇！房子變得很漂亮，像新屋啦！阿伯，你們都好嗎？」

　　「多謝志工的幫忙，環境改善就不一樣囉。兒子現在狀況也好很多，還會幫忙照顧協會的狗，很感謝你們。」阿伯謝個不停。

But Atao was very unquiet, fearing that the visitors would grab her son and take him to the hospital. She wrapped her hands tightly around her son. Dr. Chen, gently patting her son's head while looking at his medication, said to the child, "Have you helped your dad take care of stray dogs?" The boy said that he would go from time to time, and he answered several ensuing questions. Dr. Chen nodded, encouraging him to help his father more as it would be beneficial to his health.

Then Dr. Chen advised the old man to take his son to the hospital for regular check-ups, which could keep his son's condition under better control and thus making hospitalization unnecessary. The possibility of no hospitalization did magic to Atao as she slowly let go of her son.

"Atao, do you have faith in any god?"

"Yes, I am a Christian, and my husband believes in Guanyin. So two gods are looking after us for which we are very grateful."

The doctor then caught a glimpse of a wine bottle on the floor.

"I've quit drinking. Yes, I've been on the wagon. I know that if I keep drinking I will only ruin my health, and even Jesus won't love me." Atao hurriedly said. However, her son said, "Mom cries every time she drinks, and she cries so loudly that I don't dare to get near her."

倒是阿桃很緊張，怕他們抓兒子去住院，雙手緊緊地圍住兒子。陳醫師摸了摸孩子的頭，看看他的用藥狀況，接著問他幾個問題，「你有沒有幫忙爸爸照顧流浪狗？」孩子說他偶爾會去，接著幾個問題孩子也都有問有答，陳醫師點點頭，鼓勵他要多幫爸爸的忙，這樣身體會更好。

　　接著陳醫師叮嚀阿伯，要定期帶兒子到醫院檢查，這樣就不會嚴重到要住院了，阿桃一聽到不用住院，緩緩放下圈護著兒子的手臂。

　　「阿桃，你有信仰嗎？」

　　「有，我是基督徒，先生信觀世音，有兩位神明一起照顧，我們很感謝。」

　　醫師忽然瞥見地上的酒瓶……

　　「我已經戒了，戒了，我知道再喝下去身體會壞掉，耶穌也不會愛我。」阿桃搶著說。兒子一旁告狀：「媽媽每次喝酒就哭，很大聲的哭鬧喔，我都不敢靠近。」

"She's drinking very little, and she's getting better," her husband rushed to defend her.

Dr. Chen turned to Atao and said, "What does drinking mean to you? What do you feel after drinking?"

"You don't have to think about it so much because it's really easy," said Dr. Chen. "What do you usually do to pass the time?"

"Grow vegetables and melons."

"Interested? Isn't it fun?"

"It's okay. At least I can harvest and eat it to save some grocery money."

Dr. Chen gave a thumbs up, "Great! You're very considerate, doing things for the good of your family."

"That's nothing. I am worthless and a failure. It's all my fault; I can't even keep my own son," Atao said as she thought of her eldest son. Atao choked up.

"It must be awfully hard on you. I understand. The time between you and your oldest son is up, so he has gone to a better place."

"But I miss him so much. It's hard."

「她已經喝很少了，有在進步啦！」阿伯也趕緊替老婆辯解。

　　陳醫師轉頭問阿桃：「喝酒對你的意義是什麼？喝了以後有什麼感覺？」

　　「可以不用想那麼多，很輕鬆！」

　　「你平常都在做些什麼？」

　　「種菜、種瓜。」

　　「有興趣嗎？好玩嗎？」

　　「還好，起碼可以採來吃，節省開銷。」

　　陳醫師豎起大姆指：「讚啦！你很賢慧喔，都為這個家著想。」

　　「哪有？我什麼都不行，都是我不好，連孩子都守不住。」想到大兒子，阿桃哽咽了。

　　「你一定很難過，我了解，你們的緣份是有期限的，時間到了，老大到更好的地方去啦！」

　　「但我很想念他，很苦！」

"How do you ease your pain when you miss him?" Dr. Chen gently guided Atao.

"Drink, but not much now, because people don't like to see me drinking."

"What do they say about you?"

"The grandma next door couldn't stand it, and said that if I don't quit drinking, it would be better for her to just die and reincarnate."

"What will your son in heaven say when he sees you drinking?"

"He'll hate me and call me useless!"

"Your husband said you've made progress, though. What should you do now when you have an urge to drink?"

"A church sister taught me to put $100 into a piggy bank to thank the Lord whenever I feel like drinking, and then ask the Lord to help me and bless me so I may successfully quit drinking."

"Very good. Does it work for you?"

"Yes, I've been drinking less. You know why? Because money doesn't grow on trees, and it takes great effort to earn money. Furthermore, I love money!" Atao is a straight shooter.

"She has really improved a lot!" her husband hurriedly defended his wife.

「想念他的時候，你怎麼緩和自己的痛苦呢？」陳醫師溫和地引導阿桃。．

「喝酒，但現在不會喝很多了，因為大家都不喜歡我喝。」

「他們都怎麼說你呢？」

「隔壁阿媽受不了，説如果再不戒酒，還不如死死去投胎。」

「在天上的孩子看到你喝酒會怎麼説？」

「他會討厭，説我無用啦！」

「阿伯説你有進步啦，現在想喝的時候怎麼辦？」

「有師姊教我，想喝就把一百塊丟進存錢筒，感恩主，然後求主幫助我，祝福我，戒酒成功。」

「很好啊，對你有效嗎？」

「有啊，我就會喝少一點，因為錢很難賺，我很愛錢！」阿桃一點都沒心機。

「她真的進步很多啦！」阿伯趕緊替太太辯解。

"It's good to be making progress, and if it's effective, you have to continue to do it. Your deceased son, in fact, has not really disappeared, but rather he just exists in another form. You have to pick yourself up. Use your love for your oldest son to love yourself. You have to forgive yourself for the loss of your son. In addition to thanking God, you also have to thank yourself. You have done your best, so let go of the past and move on. Be a good mother, and be a good example for your younger son as surely he will be learning from you." Atao quietly nodded her consent and promise.

Then Dr. Chen taught Atao simple exercises to relieve stress. He told her to do them at least 20 times a day, and she did as she was told.

Dr. Chen was now feeling much better about Atao, and he continued to use her younger son to cheer Atao up: "Your youngest son may not always be with you. If you continue to crave drinking all the time, maybe you, not your son, will have to go to the hospital for treatment. You must earnestly quit drinking so that your son will feel at ease to live with you, and you must be his role model."

"If she needs to go to the hospital, I'll give her a ride," Atao's loving husband said.

「有在進步很好啊，有效就要繼續做。逝去的人，其實並沒有真正消失，他只是換另一種形式存在，你要振作起來，以他的愛，好好愛自己，你要原諒自己的失去，除了感恩神，也要跟自己說感恩，你已經盡力了，要放下過去繼續往前走，做一位好媽媽，做小兒子的好榜樣，他會學你喔。」聽著陳醫師的話，阿桃默默地點點頭。

接著陳醫師教阿桃做釋壓的簡單運動，說「每天至少要做二十次喔」，她乖乖地跟著做。

陳醫師放心多了，繼續用「兒子」給阿桃打氣：「小兒子不是永遠都可以待在你身邊，如果你還是一直想喝酒的話，也許換成是你要去住院接受治療喔。你一定要認真把酒戒掉，兒子才會放心跟你住一起啊，你要做他的榜樣。」

「如果需要去醫院治療，我會載她去。」疼老婆的阿伯搶著說。

"No, I will diligently exercise. For the sake of my oldest son in heaven, and to be a role model for the children around me, I will drink no more–cross my heart." Atao said solemnly.

The setting sun shone on Xiaoshu, Dr. Chen, and the team leader on their way home, "The most feared thing in the world is regret and loss. To avoid regrets, people use all ways imaginable to escape such emotions; in Atao's case, she uses alcohol to numb herself. Fortunately she is grateful, and that can gradually alleviate her suffering."

Observing the change in his own mood from the time he lost his billfold and the period after that, Xiaoshu said, "When my wallet was stolen, I lost all the money I had with me, NT$300, and I couldn't take the public transportation because my ride pass was stolen, too. At that time, I felt that I owned nothing in this whole world, and I felt just lousy. But then I practiced the mental game of 'seeing the bright side in everything in life' to change my state of mind, and I was pleasantly surprised that things began to really go well for me. And after learning about the pain Atao has had to endure for the loss of her oldest son and the worry of losing another son, I deeply appreciate that she is suffering real and incomparable pain. By comparison, my own loss of $10 is nothing, almost

「不用啦，我會認真做運動，為了天上的孩子，還有做身邊孩子的榜樣，我不會再喝啦！真的。」阿桃很用力地說。

　　夕陽照在小樹、陳醫師與隊長的回家路上，「人世間最怕的是後悔與失去，因為怕失去，而用許多方法來逃離這樣的情緒，阿桃用喝酒來麻痺自己，還好她有感恩的心，可以逐漸減輕她的苦。」

　　想起錢包被偷當時和之後的心境轉變，小樹分享：「當我錢包被偷，身上僅有的三百元也同時失去，也沒了車票無法搭車回家，當時只覺得自己一無所有，那種瞬間跌落谷底的失落情緒差點轉不過來。但我後來運用『凡事往好處想』的心念練習，讓自己轉變心境，沒想到事情也確實往好的方向發展。而且在知道阿桃失去孩子的痛，和擔憂再次失去的憂慮之後，我才深刻理解，

laughable. Seeing other's suffering helps me appreciate how blessed I have been, so I have to learn to be grateful."

"Right. In addition to the practice of 'seeing the bright side in everything in life', try the game of 'nothing to your name', which stimulates you to think of a creative solution when you are caught between a rock and a hard place. In your case, practice to accept the fact that that NT$300 is no longer your money and–importantly–also practice to empathize with the person who is so poor as to need to take a mere NT$300 from you. Positive thinking is the best way to divert painful emotions," the team leader said. Xiaoshu couldn't agree with him more because positive thinking helped him achieve exactly that, and may have helped him recover the stolen billfold.

Atao's family is poor, afflicted with disease, and has lost a loved one. "In fact, there is no fairness in the world to speak of. The important thing is to be grateful. I have seen some husbands run away when their wives are sick, or when their children have physical and mental disabilities, and I have also seen some wives, after finding out that their husbands are seriously ill, take their husband's money and leave forever. Although the family we visited today is imperfect, they still stick together."

那才真的是無法比擬的傷痛。我們真的要見苦知福，要學會感恩。」

「嗯，除了『凡事往好處想』的練習，這還是『一無所有』的試煉，就是讓你再想辦法，在面臨困境時激出創意，接受三百元不再屬於你的事實，同時也釋出了善意幫助那需要三百元的人。正向思考，是轉移痛苦情緒的最佳方法。」小樹對小隊長的話深表贊同，因為自己做到了，可能也因此找回了被偷的錢包。

回想阿伯這一家人，又窮又病還失去所愛，「其實人世間本就沒有公平可言，重要的是要有一顆感謝的心，我看過有的老公見老婆生病，或者兒女身心有障礙就逃家不敢面對，也有老婆發現老公身染重病就捲款離家，今天這個家庭雖然有所殘缺，但他們還是很努力地過日子。」

The fact of the matter is that gaining is not necessarily a blessing, and losing is not necessarily a curse. Atao's husband, optimistic and cheerful, is a perfect example of positive thinking: do not evade responsibilities, which he faces directly and optimistically. He will bring strength and courage to his family, which they need in order to move forward in their lives.

其實，得到未必是福，失去也未必是禍。阿伯樂觀開朗的性格，恰是最好的正向磁場，不逃避，直接且樂觀面對，會帶給家人繼續走下去的力量與勇氣。

The Magic of A Positive Attitude

Too much negative thinking leads to mental fatigues.
Positive thinking ends the ill effects of negative thinking.
The capacity of the heart is limited. Too many negative emotions
leaves little room in the heart for joy.
Life can't be perfect, so don't be too harsh to yourself.
Life's biggest enemy is emotions spinned out of control.
Positive thinking will lead you to happiness and shield you
from suffering.

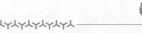

正能量的磁場效應

心累，是因有太多的負面情緒在內耗
正向思考才會有負面的停損點
心的容量有限，裝了太多負面情緒，歡喜進不去了
人生不可能完美，不用太苛刻對待自己
人生最大的敵人是失控的情緒
正向思考會讓我們離苦得樂

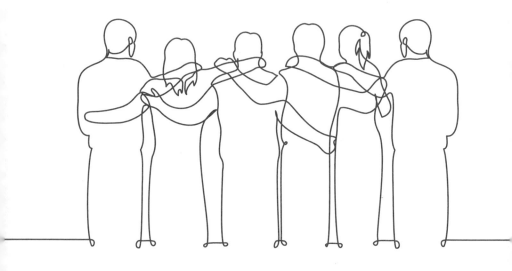

第四章
CHAPTER 4

事件是來保護你的

Things happened to protect you

Jingli and Xiaoshu are on the same volunteer team. One day, Xiaoshu received a call from Jingli. "Last Saturday, we went to the long-term care center to volunteer. Why didn't you go?" Jingli said.

"Well, no one had informed me. Did you go?"

"Of course!"

Xiaoshu was a little lost when he heard this. It's unusual that Team Leader Wu didn't invite him, and the event wasn't announced to the group. Could it be announced to another group, of which he was not a member? He felt annoyed and slighted. He felt ostracized.

"I was going to pick your brains on something that day." Jingli said.

Xiaoshu, still suspicious, looked at his phone and said, "There was no group notification of the event. How did the team leader notify you?"

"Oh, I just happened to meet him in the studio, and he told me."

"Maybe I should call the team leader and ask why he didn't invite me?"

一天，小樹接到志工組隊友靜麗打來的電話：「上星期六我們去長照中心當志工，你怎麼沒來呀？」

　　「沒有耶，沒有人通知我啊。妳有去嗎？」

　　「當然有！」

　　小樹聽了有點失落，「奇怪，吳小隊長怎麼沒邀我？群組也沒傳，難道有另一個群組？」被忽視的感覺很不開心，還多疑到是否被人刻意排除在外。

　　「我本來有點事要請教你的。」靜麗說。

　　還在狐疑的小樹，看了看手機，「群組沒傳啊，那小隊長怎麼通知你的？」

　　「喔，剛好我去畫室遇到他，他告訴我的。」

　　「也許我該打電話問問小隊長，為何沒邀我？」

Not long after hanging up the phone, a call came through. This time it was from someone at the household registration office asking to verify Xiaoshu's name and ID number, because a visitor to that office was using his name to apply for a household registration transcript. "Wow, I myself don't even know about this matter. Why would I apply for a household registration transcript when I have no business doing that? Who is that person? Would you get him to talk to me?" said Xiaoshu. Someone on the other end of the phone called Xiaoshu's name, and soon the household registration office officer came back to the phone and said, "That person vanished."

"That's good. Thanks for your alertness to stop this nonsense just in time," Xiaoshu said and was about to hang up the phone. "Wait, you can't just forget it, you have to report this incident to the police. I'll give you the phone number for the police station in your precinct." After hanging up the phone, Xiaoshu thought about it some more and decided to pay a visit to the household registration office to identify the impersonator.

As soon as he entered the elevator, he received a call from the police and asked him if he wanted to report the crime. When Xiaoshu explained to the caller, a person next to him in

掛斷電話沒多久，電話又來了，是戶政事務所的人打來的，說要核對小樹的名字與身分證字號是否正確，因為現場有人用他的名字要申請戶口謄本，「哇，我本人都不知道有這件事，我沒事幹麼要申請戶口謄本？那個人是誰？請他來跟我說話好嗎？」電話那頭有人直呼小樹的名字，不久，電話那頭的人又回來說，「那個人不見了……」

「那就好，還好你們及時發現，謝謝。」小樹正要掛電話，「等等，你不可以這樣就算了，要去報警，向警方報案才對啊！來，我給你所屬轄區的警方電話是……」掛斷電話，小樹想想，還是去一趟戶政事務所再次確認，到底是哪個人冒用他的名字。

剛進電梯，就接到警方打來，問他要報案嗎？小樹在電梯裡向對方說明時，旁邊一位同搭電梯的人拍拍他

the elevator patted him on the shoulder and whispered, "That's a scam. Ignore it." "I'll call you later." Xiaoshu quickly came to his senses, saved the caller number, and hung up the phone.

At the household registration office, Xiaoshu took out his ID card and other documents to identify himself. The household registration officer said that, because of a suspected data breach, many people had been targeted by scammers who further acquired the personal information of the family members of those people. The scammers then use all such stolen personal information to open accounts at financial institutions to conduct fraudulent financial transactions. They can even imitate your voice to make calls. They can do pretty much whatever they want to do. Even the household registration office has difficulties identifying and stopping all the scammers. Everyone should keep their eyes and ears open.

After listening to the officer's warning, Xiaoshu was a little annoyed. The team leader who should have called didn't call, and the one who shouldn't have called did actually call and tried to deceive him. Walking out of the household registration office, Xiaoshu turned into an alley to go home. When he was about to get home, a young man of Xiaoshu's age approached him. At first glance, the man looked a little familiar, but

的肩，小聲地說，「那是詐騙，別理。」「我等下打給你。」小樹很快會意過來，把來電號碼儲存下來，然後掛了電話。

來到戶政事務所確認，小樹拿出身分證等證件核對時，果然，戶政人員說，因為疑似個資外洩，很多人都被詐騙集團盯上，這些人有了個資，再來會進一步要你家人的個資，把你當人頭，模仿你的聲音來電，就能為所欲為，「我們也防不勝防，大家要各自小心。」

聽完，小樹有點煩。該打電話的小隊長沒打來，不該打的竟打來想騙他。走出戶政機關彎進小巷，快到家時，一名跟小樹年紀相仿的年輕人靠了過來，乍看有點

Xiaoshu couldn't exactly place the man.

"You are Xiaoshu, right? I'm Anxu. Your mom just drove and hit a pedestrian, and now she is in a hospital. She needs money to give to the injured party. She is very anxious, and she asked me to find you. Please quickly transfer money to my account, and I will take it to her for the emergency." Xiaoshu was stunned for a moment, and he subconsciously checked his pocket. Oops, his billfold was gone! Although he was a little flustered, he still managed to call his mother, but she didn't answer. He took a deep breath to calm himself. Then he tried to sense, but he couldn't sense his mother's anxiety. Next he sensed this Anxu stranger who seemed somewhat familiar. Xiaoshu sensed that Anxu, standing opposite himself, was in a state of confusion. Xiaoshu now realized what was going on. He fished for things in his pocket, and said to this Anxu person, "Wait just a minute. My wallet is missing, so I have to call my bank." In fact, at this time, Xiaoshu took the opportunity to call the anti-fraud center.

Soon, the police arrived, and Anxu started to run away. But he hadn't gone very far before the police arrested and handcuffed him. The police told Xiaoshu that Anxu was just a runner for scammers.

面熟，但一時想不起他是誰。

「你是小樹吧？我是安旭。你媽媽剛才開車撞了路人，現在人在醫院，需要一筆錢給對方，她很急，要我來找你，請你趕緊轉錢給我，我帶去給她救急。」小樹一下子愣住了，下意識摸摸口袋，糟糕，錢包居然不見了！雖然有點慌亂，他還是趕緊打電話給媽媽，沒接，他深吸了一口氣，將煩亂的心定下來，試著去感應，但感應不到媽媽的焦躁，於是直接試著感應這名陌生又有點面熟的人；小樹感覺到對面這個人內心一片混沌，他有點明白了，摸摸口袋，很機警地跟這個人說，「等一下，我錢包不見了，得打電話給銀行。」其實，這會兒小樹是利用機會打給反詐騙中心。

不久，警察來了，這名年輕人一看就跑，但很快被警員給追上了，也上了銬，警察告訴小樹，對方是詐騙的車手。

Only then did it dawn on Xiaoshu that Anxi was indeed his classmate in elementary school. Anxu was one of those kids who often gave the teacher a headache. He always waited for free lunch every day. Xiaoshu also remembered that he often collected protection money from weak classmates. Once his grandfather went to school and asked him why he collected protection money from his classmates and scared them so much that they refused to go to school. Anxu said, "Why do they all have pocket money, but only I don't? That's why it's only fair for them to give me some of their money!" The answer totally silenced his grandfather. It was said that the grandfather would squeeze out a little money every week for this precious grandson.

Xiaoshu tagged along as the police took Anxu to the police station for booking. At this time, a middle-aged woman came into the station to report a case. She was crying loudly, saying that her mother was going to have surgery, so she went to her bank to get some money only to find out that someone else had already withdrawn from her bank account down to zero. She was at a loss. Her loud wailing convinced the officer to turn his attention to her. Xiaoshu took this opportunity to ask Anxu, "I'm curious. How did you know that my mother wouldn't

小樹這時才想起，他真的是小學的同學，那個在班上常常狐假虎威讓老師頭痛的安旭，記得他每天都在等著吃免費的午餐便當。小樹還想起他常跟弱小的同學收保護費，有一次他爺爺來學校，問他為何跟同學收保護費，害人家不敢來上學？安旭居然還跟爺爺嗆聲：「為什麼他們都有零用錢，只有我沒有？所以他們要分一些給我才公平啊！」窮困的爺爺默然了，聽說後來爺爺每星期都會擠出一點點錢給這寶貝孫。

　　小樹跟著警察，帶著安旭來到派出所做筆錄，這時，一名中年婦女來報案，大聲哭說，她娘家母親要開刀，這才發現銀行帳戶被盜領光，不知怎麼辦才好？哭聲好淒厲，警方轉頭處理婦人的事，小樹這時問安旭：「我很好奇，你怎麼知道我媽不會接電話？」

answer the phone?"

"Because someone had called her before you did, and he kept calling until she couldn't stand it anymore and turned off her phone. And then I was instructed to approach you."

"I'm curious, where did you work after graduation?" Xiaoshu asked.

"I went wherever there was money to be made. My grandfather is bedridden, and now he needs a lot of money in a hurry. I don't have any choice. You are lucky to have loving parents to you."

The policeman beside them couldn't help but interject: "Suppose someone else's grandparents are sick and the money they need for treatment has been cheated out by someone like you, therefore they do not get the treatment. Is it okay with you?" the officer continued, "Do you want to steal some money now and be on the run forever? Do you want to live a life like that? Who's the boss behind you? Who told you to do this?"

"I don't know who the boss is. All I care about is that I get paid. I got caught today; blame it on my lousy luck. At most I get locked up, and that's no no big deal." Anxu said, not giving a hoot.

「因為有人先打電話給你媽媽，而且會不斷來電直到你媽媽不堪其擾而關機，然後我就接到指示來找你。」

「我很好奇，你畢業後都在哪裡工作？」小樹問。

「哪裡有錢賺就去哪，我爺爺臥病在床，現在急需要很多錢，我又沒得選擇。不像你，有疼愛你的雙親能幫你。」

一旁的警察聽了忍不住插嘴：「那別人的爺爺奶奶生病了，錢被騙光了，沒得醫治，就沒關係嗎？」警察邊做筆錄邊說：「你是想要騙一筆錢，然後跑給警察追，天涯海角地跑，你想過這樣的日子嗎？你的幕後老闆是誰？是誰指使你這樣做的？」

「我也不知道老闆是誰，反正只要拿到錢就好了，被抓到算我倒霉，頂多被關，沒什麼大不了。」安旭一副不在乎。

"I know you can't care less if you're locked up, but what about your loved ones like your grandfather? He will be sad and disappointed in you; you will hurt the people whom you deceived. Some of the money you stole is money that people must have in order to save their lives, like the lady who just now cried so miserably. Can you imagine how severe the damage is? Haven't you thought about the damaging effects of your action on the victims?" the officer said. "This is your first offense, and you didn't succeed, so you may not need to go to jail. But if you break the law again, the punishment will definitely be more severe. What's more, God is watching, and he won't let you get away with it." Having probably caught countless fledgling scam drivers, the police earnestly admonished Anxu.The more the police talked, the more Anxu lowered his head and the less he spoke to defend himself. Then an old man came in, limping with a cane and uttering hoarsely, "Anxu, Anxu, is that you? What's the trouble this time?"

At the sight of the old man, Anxu immediately asked the police officer to get up and help steady the old man. "Grandpa, why are you here? Why are you not at home? What are you doing here?"

"You're in trouble again? The police called me."

「你覺得自己被關沒什麼，但是你周圍的親人，你爺爺怎麼辦呢？他對你會傷心會失望，還有被你騙的人，都會受到傷害，你們騙來的，有些是人家的救命錢，像剛才那位太太哭得那麼淒慘，那傷害有多大，難道你都沒想過別人要怎麼辦嗎？你是初犯，加上沒有得逞，可能還不至於吃牢飯，但是你若要再犯，一旦有犯罪事實，那肯定會加重刑罰。何況老天爺都在看，更不會放過你的！」大概已抓過無數初出茅廬的詐騙車手，警察忿忿不平地諄諄以教。隨著警察的話語，安旭越聽頭越低，也不再出言抗辯。這時候來了一位老人，拄著手杖一拐一拐地，聲音沙啞地喊著：「小旭、小旭在哪裡？又闖什麼禍了？」

　　安旭一看是爺爺，趕緊向警察請求起身去攙扶老人，「爺爺你怎麼會來？怎麼不在家，來這做什麼？」

　　「你又闖禍了？是警察叫我來的。」

"No problem, Grandpa. Go home and get some rest." Anxu turned to glare at the police officer and said, "My grandfather's condition is life-threatening, and you have the heart to call him to come over? What if anything goes wrong with him?" The old man was blustering and panting, so the officer took a few quick steps forward to help him sit down.

"Anxu, you mustn't do anything that is not allowed. Otherwise, I will turn in my grave," Grandpa gasped and angrily chided Anxu.

"Everything is fine. It's all a misunderstanding, Grandpa. You see that Xiaoshu,the genius in our class, is also there?" said Anxu, seeking help from Xiaoshu.

"Grandpa Li, Anxu told me that you are unwell and need surgery, right?" Xiaoshu said.

"It's no use. I'm just old, and surgery will do no good. I told Anxu several times that I don't need it. You have to teach him and help him to be a contributing member of society. That is more important than me getting surgery."

"Many kind-hearted people and charities are ready to help the needy. If you need help, just apply through established channels, Anxu. Never make money in a way that harms others

「沒事沒事，爺爺趕緊回去休息，我沒事。」安旭轉頭瞪著警察，「我爺爺的病會危及生命，你們有沒有人性？還要通知他過來？萬一路上發生什麼事，你們要不要負責？」警員看安旭的爺爺臉紅氣喘，也趕緊協助扶他坐下。

「小旭呀，你不能做出天理不容的事喔！不然爺爺死不瞑目。」爺爺喘吁吁很生氣地責備安旭。

「沒事沒事，是誤會啦。爺爺你沒看到我們班的天才小樹也在呀？」小旭向小樹釋出求救的眼神。

「李爺爺，聽說您生病了需要開刀是嗎？」小樹關懷地問。

「沒用啦，老了就是老了，開刀也沒用，我跟小旭講了好幾次不需要啦。你要好好教教他，要做社會上有用的人，這比讓我去開刀更重要。」

「現在社會上有很多善心人士、慈善團體可以幫忙救助急難貧困，應該要循正常管道去申請幫助，安旭同學，千萬不要用損人不利己的方式去賺錢，犯罪的人最

and yourself. Criminals are destined to be locked up in the end," said the police officer.

"The officer is right. You can't commit crimes anymore," Xiaoshu said to Anxu. "Have you considered any legitimate work? I'll try to help you out."

"I just don't want to depend on others anymore. I have never had dignity since I was a child. Everyone looks down on me. I want to use my own labor to make money to support my grandfather. I want to show others that I can," Anxu said angrily.

"Cheating people out of their money will only make others look down on you more. Hurting innocent people is not only against the law, it is also undignified!" said the police officer.

"But I don't have any professional skills. I'm useless, so how will any people want to hire me?" Anxu continued to complain.

Images of how Anxu used to behave in their elementary school suddenly came vividly back into Xiaoshu's mind. "By the way, Anxu, you were the courageous one in our class. Remember? On one rainy day our classmate Chubby fell down on the playground. An ensuing nosebleed scared everyone to death, but not you. Without saying a word, you just picked him up and ran in the heavy rain to the infirmary for first

後注定是要吃牢籠飯的。」警員再次警告安旭。

「警察先生說得很對，你真的不能再做這種犯罪的事了。你有想到什麼正當工作嗎？我設法幫你打聽看怎麼幫上你。」小樹跟安旭說。

「我只是不想再靠別人，從小就沒有尊嚴，沒有人看得起我，我想用自己的力量賺錢養爺爺，我要做給別人看。」安旭忿忿說著。

「選擇用騙人的方式賺錢，會更讓人瞧不起。傷害無辜的人，不僅天理不容，更找不回尊嚴！」警察忍不住又說了。

「但我沒有專業能力，根本一無是處，是個沒用的人，哪有工作會要我！」安旭繼續怨懟。

小樹想起同學小時候的事，「對了，安旭，你很有勇氣，你還記得嗎？當時班上同學呆胖下雨天在操場摔倒，鼻血直流，我們擔心害怕不知該怎麼辦？是你二話不說就揹起他，不顧劈頭暴雨就往醫務室跑，雖然事後也沒人獎賞你，但我一直記得，你好有勇氣、好有力氣、也好有義氣，呆胖又重又愛哭，當時瘦小的你居然氣都不喘，揹著他穿越整個操場一路跑到醫務室，你那奮勇

aid. Although no one bothered to reward you, I will always remember that you were so courageous, so powerful, and so righteous. Chubby was chubby, heavy, and whining, and you were very skinny at that time. But you didn't even get out of breath after that long sprint through the entire playground to the infirmary. Your spirit of fighting to save people is really admirable," said Xiaoshu. Anxu scratched his head and said bashfully, "Oh, I forgot. You still remember?"During the conversation Xiaoshu picked up an incoming call from Team Leader Wu. "I didn't invite you to the long-term care center last time because you didn't fit the need that day. They were short on manual labor, so I took some people over for them to try out. Because you don't need the work, so I didn't invite you."

"It's such a coincidence, I have a friend here who needs to work, and he is very strong and loving," Xiaoshu said, looking at Anxu, and Anxu nodded.

"Of course. You can bring him here at any time. They have a real labor shortage here."

"By the way, this friend's grandfather needs surgery and their family needs help. Do you know of a charity that provides assistance to elderly and poor families?"

救人的精神真令人佩服。」安旭搔搔頭：「我都忘了，你怎麼記得？」談話間鈴聲響起，小樹接起手機，是吳小隊長來電：「上次沒邀你去長照中心，是因為他們缺職工，那是體力活，所以要我帶人去給他們測試力氣，因為你不需要工作，所以就沒找你。」

「這麼巧，我現在這裡有朋友需要工作，他力氣很大又有愛心。」小樹望向安旭，安旭點點頭。

「可以啊，那你方便隨時可以帶他過來，這裡真的很缺人。」

「對了對了，我這朋友的爺爺生病需要開刀，因為家境關係需要幫助，你知道有提供高齡貧病家庭援助的慈善團體嗎？」

"Yes, as long as they passed the confirmation and evaluation, it's usually no problem." The police officer was very happy to hear that. He said, "Anxu, now you have a proper job, and your grandfather's medical expenses have also been taken care of. They are all your benefactors, and you need to cherish them all."

"Yes, they are all my great benefactors. It seems that I have never met any benefactors before now." Anxu was very moved.

A woman, who looked like a police officer, interrupted: "Don't think that way. Benefactors are all over the place in life. People and events around us, good or bad, are all our benefactors. We just need to be mindful and seek them out. Even diseases are our benefactors." The police officer introduced the woman as "Teacher Guan," who was in charge of psychological counseling at the police station.

"How is that possible? Having contracted diseases is very unfortunate, so how can diseases be benefactors?" Anxu wasn't convinced.

"Because illness can promote our health awareness, psychological growth, and self-reflection. It can also improve interpersonal relationships. People often rely on others for support in the face of illness, which lends itself to strengthening

「有啊，只要經過評估確認，通常都沒有問題。」警員在旁聽了也很高興，「安旭同學，這下你有正當工作了，爺爺的醫療費用也有著落了，他們都是你的貴人，你要好好珍惜。」

「會的，大貴人。我好像生平第一次遇到貴人。」安旭很感動。

這時一位貌似女警的人聽到安旭的話，忍不住走了過來：「你不能這麼想。其實人生到處有貴人，我們周遭的人事物，無論正面或負面的都是貴人，只是我們不常去發覺而已，甚至連疾病也都是我們的貴人。」做筆錄的警察趕緊介紹，原來她是在警局裡專責心理諮商輔導的「關老師」。

「怎麼可能？得了疾病就很不幸了，怎麼能說疾病是貴人。」安旭難掩疑惑。

「因為疾病能推動我們健康意識的提高、心理成長和自我反思。還可以改善人際關係：在面對疾病時，人

ties between family and friends. People who are sick may become more grateful to others for their love and support, which can lead to deep emotional connections. Anxu, your grandfather is sick, so don't you feel that you care more about your grandfather now? Doesn't your grandpa's illness lead us to this gathering here today? Also, historically, there have been many medical and technological breakthroughs that have been born out of the need to fight disease. Necessity is the mother of invention. Needs are more likely to inspire innovative solutions and products for human beings, so won't you say that diseases are our benefactors?

Everyone fell silent for a long while. Then grandpa nodded in agreement: "From that perspective, Anxu's mistake this time is also God's way to help him self-reflect. I'm ashamed that I didn't teach Anxu well, and his attempt at scamming has brought nothing but trouble to you all. But, on the other hand, I'm also very grateful that he got such a great lesson because of this incident. I am thoroughly grateful." Grandpa cried as he spoke and nodded his appreciation to everyone.

Xiaoshu's mobile phone rang again, and this time it was from the household registration office. The caller said, "You forgot your wallet here. Please be sure to come and pick it up."

們常依賴他人的支持，這有助於加強家庭和朋友之間的聯繫。患病者可能更加感恩他人的關愛，這都可以促進雙方深厚的情感聯繫。安旭，你爺爺生病了，你不是因此更關心爺爺了嗎？甚至於這次事件不也都是為了爺爺的病嗎？還有，從歷史上來看，有許多醫學和科技的突破都是由於對抗疾病的需求而誕生的，因為『有需要』，就更能激發出人類的創新解決方案和產品，你說，疾病算不算是貴人呢？」

聽完她的一番話，大家陷入一片沉默，爺爺在旁點頭，「這樣說起來，小旭這次犯錯也是老天來幫他自我反省啊！很慚愧，我沒有教好小旭，讓他搭上騙局還麻煩到你們。但也很感謝，讓他因此得到這麼棒的教育，真是感恩啊！」爺爺邊講邊落淚，還頻頻向大家致意。

此時，小樹的手機鈴聲又響起，是戶政事務所打來的，「你的錢包忘在這裡了，請記得回來領取！」

Is it a scam or not this time? Xiaoshu was a little suspicious and a little mixed up. After repeated verification with the caller, Xiaoshu was certain that he had left his wallet there. With suspicion lifted, Xiaoshu became deep in thought: "I think the biggest sin of the fraud syndicate is to destroy the trust between people, which is difficult to restore. It is a must to re-establish mutual trust."

Therapist Guan also said, "I hope that young people can form a value system, not pursue profit at the expense of their conscience and morality, adhere to the basic values of human nature, and choose kindness and altruism. Then our society can have hope, peace, and harmony. As a living being, one must be grateful and do things to give back to heaven and earth."

As the saying goes, "Good people are bullied by other people, but not by heaven. Conversely, evil people are feared by other people, but not by heaven." This may well be the moral of this story for everyone who was involved in this fraud.

這次是真的嗎？小樹有點狐疑，腦筋一時有點轉不過來。經過再三確認，錢包確實是忘在那了。放下心中疑慮，小樹心有所感：「我覺得詐騙集團最大的罪過，是摧毀了人與人之間的信任，這很難逆轉，很需要重新建立起彼此的互信！」

　　「關老師」也說：「希望年輕人都可以建立起一種價值觀，不因為追求利益而喪失良心和道德，並且堅持人性的基本價值，選擇善良與利他，這樣我們的社會才有希望祥和。人能活著，除了要感恩，總還要做一些回饋天地的事啊。」

　　正所謂「人善人欺天不欺，人惡人怕天不怕。」這該是被捲進這回詐騙事件的眾人，心裡共同的體悟吧！

The Magic of A Positive Attitude

If you don't change your negative thinking, your future will
become black and white!
Instead of desperately trying to forget the bad memories, it is
better to reconstruct good memories for yourself.
If your mind still stays in the past or jumps to the future,
Merely allowing your mind to go back to the present moment can
alleviate your uneasiness and pain.
If you don't feel like you're good enough, you still have hope in
your heart.
Make the heart stronger, and time will repair the emotional scars.

正能量的磁場效應

一直不改變負面思考，未來會變成一片黑白！

與其拚命想忘掉不好記憶，不如重編好的回憶給自己

如果心仍在「過去」或跳往「未來」

只要讓思緒回到當下，就能減輕不安和痛苦

如果你覺得自己不夠好，代表心中還抱持著希望

讓內心變得更強大，時間會修復情緒黑洞

第五章
CHAPTER 5

當自己的啦啦隊

Be your own cheerleader

The thought of cousin Xiaomei suddenly popped into Xiaoshu's mind after he had finished breakfast one day, and immediately felt a faint but deep pain near his heart, as if he had been wronged and oppressed.

He turned on his computer and did a quick mental scan of recent postings in the online community of him and his cousins. Many of them shared how they were doing. Xiaoshu noticed that cousin Xiaomei was either absent from the chats or was a quiet participant; she sometimes just joined the chat only to exit soon after. Xiaoshu raised his concerns, but his cousins mostly brushed them aside, believing that Xiaomei, a social worker, was just overwhelmed by her caseload so much so that she couldn't find time to chat.

However, Xiaoshu felt that things might be more complicated than that. He sensed that Xiaomei was engulfed in a big wave of powerlessness and fatigue. It seemed that she was losing her fighting spirit fast and an unseen dark hand was pressing on her and making her unable to breathe; she was powerless to resist.

He couldn't help but frequently call Xiaomei to plead with her to turn on the video conferencing. It took a long time for Xiaomei to finally appear on the computer screen.

小樹今天一早起床吃完早餐後，忽然想起堂姊曉梅，馬上覺得身體悶悶的，似乎心口附近有著隱約深沉的痛，好像有什麼委屈壓抑在血管裡流動翻攪著。

　　他打開電腦，腦海浮現昨晚跟幾位堂表兄弟姊妹在網路社群上分享彼此近況，小樹主動關心為何曉梅堂姊好一陣子不是缺席沒上線，就是上線了也老是潛水不出聲，過沒多久就下線這件事。其他人覺得小樹想太多，當社工的曉梅應該是最近個案太多，忙昏了，所以抽不出時間聊天。

　　不過，小樹覺得事情可能沒這麼單純。他感應到有一種深沉疲累的無力感，伴隨著鼓不起勇氣與鬥志的倦怠感襲來，血液彷彿逆流，快無法呼吸了，像似有隻黑暗的大手，正使出蠻力狠狠壓迫著，叫人無力抵抗。

　　他忍不住頻頻呼叫曉梅開啟視訊。經過好一陣子，曉梅才終於出現在電腦螢幕上。

"Xiaomei, it's a holiday and the weather is nice, so why aren't you out taking a stroll?"

Seeing Xiaomei's listless eyes and gloomy complexion, Xiaoshu felt that his instinct about her was correct.

"I don't feel like it. A little tired," Xiaomei said, not really feeling like answering.

"I'm curious. You have seemed to be tired lately. Are you in trouble or things are not going well? You can tell me; whatever I hear stays with me. I'm here to listen and at most give some advice, but I will never spread gossip." Xiaoshu felt that he ought to show his concern timely and clearly. Xiaomei sighed and said,

"The news media and public opinion had a lot of bad things to say about social workers a while back, didn't they? To be honest, I feel a little sad because we have been smeared for no reason at all. I've always felt that those were prejudices and unverified rumors and tried to ignore them as such, but how can I totally ignore them when I face strange looks and hostile language?"

"I know," Xiaoshu said, "I understand your grievances.

「曉梅姊，今天天氣不錯，又是假日，你沒有出門走走？」

看到曉梅兩眼無光、氣色灰暗的模樣，小樹覺得自己的感應應該無誤。

「沒心情，有點累。」曉梅強打起精神，不怎麼想回答的模樣。

「姊，我很好奇，你最近看起來很累，是否有遇到麻煩的事或生活不順心？你可以跟我說啊，我小樹是個標準的好樹洞，我就負責聽，最多給點意見，但絕不會亂傳八卦喔。」小樹覺得關心要及時，單刀直入。曉梅聽了嘆口氣說：

「前陣子新聞跟輿論不是對社工有很多不好的評論嗎？老實說，我覺得莫名其妙地被黑了、有點難過，總覺得那些都是偏見跟未經求證的謠言，儘管這樣告訴自己安慰自己，但是當面對異樣的眼光和不友善的口氣，哪可能都不在乎！」

「我懂。」小樹點頭強調，「我懂姊你的委屈。我

I think that being a social worker requires a high level of empathy and sincere care–no small task by any means. I really admire social workers, who, like police, doctors, judges and other professionals, must have a strong sense of responsibility and justice. And they must be tenacious."

"Not only must social workers work hard for the lives of others, but they also must stand up to scrutiny. That's really hard work," Xiaomei continued to pour out what had been troubling her, "I attended a class reunion the other day, and that gave me an even deeper appreciation of how hurtful those criticisms could be."

Xiaomei felt that she had been terribly wronged. She recalled that on the day of the class reunion, she was very happy to see her old classmates whom she had not seen for many years. But as soon as someone started the topic of social workers, everyone piled on their criticism of social workers. Xiaomei felt exceedingly lousy.

Here are some examples of their criticisms. "Why do you want to be a social worker? Other people are making a ton of money, living in big houses and cars, and carrying fanciest brands of bags. Now, look at you. How old are you now? And you're still busy visiting cases all day?"

覺得要當社工需要很高的同理心和真誠的關懷，這很不簡單，我真的很佩服社工，需要有像警察、醫生、法官等專業人士的責任感和正義感，更要有堅韌的個性。」

「社工不僅要能為他人的生命而努力，還要有願意接受被檢視的抗壓力，想想真的是太辛苦了。」曉梅繼續把心中的煩惱倒出來，「前幾天我參加同學聚會，更深刻了解那些批評有多令人難以忍受。」

曉梅很委屈，她回想同學會那天，能見到多年不見的老同學原本非常開心，結果有人話題一開，眾人竟七嘴八舌地評論社工，讓人聽了心情超差：

「為什麼要當社工？人家都是薪水越賺賺多，房子車子越換越大，手上包包的品牌越來越響亮！都幾歲了，你還整天忙進忙出訪視個案？」

"Social workers do hard jobs, and you often become belittled targets of the news media. You are doing thankless work. You remember how fierce online postings were on social workers? Is it worth it? They work long hours, and I think this kind of work is quite dangerous and stressful. It's just not worth it."

"Yes, it feels great when you are able to find resources to help your clients, but it's hard to put up with their emotions and offer them catharsis."

Xiaomei said in exasperation to Xiaoshu, "Their complaints and commentary seemingly rushed blood to my head, blocked my arteries, and constricted my respiratory system."

"I know how it feels, and I feel it."

"In the face of overwhelming doubts, I feel powerless and about to die," Xiaomei said, her face becoming ever gloomier.

"Slanting can't disparage righteous acts," Xiaoshu said, trying his best to help his cousin rid of negative thoughts. "Pay no heed to what others are saying about your work, which they know next to nothing about. You'll go crazy if you're always concerned about other people's opinions."

Deep in thought, Xiaomei fell silent for a moment.

Xiaoshu, though, had a thought of his own, a flash of inspiration. He said, "Instead of staying at home and feeling

「當社工很辛苦，還會上報紙上新聞被罵，吃力不討好！你沒看前陣子網路罵得多兇，值得嗎？我覺得這種工作挺危險的，壓力大，工時又長，真的很不划算！」

「能幫助個案尋找可申請的資源這點是挺厲害的，不過如果還要承接案主的情緒，還要提供宣洩抒發的管道，那未免太累人了！」

「聽了這些話，我第一時間的反應是血往頭頂衝，心裡好像被什麼東西堵住，呼吸也變得困難，感覺很難受！」曉梅神情十分沮喪。

「我懂那種感覺，我也感應到了！」

「面對排山倒海而來的質疑，我覺得自己毫無招架之力，快滅頂啦！」曉梅臉色愈來愈黯淡。

「人家說身正不怕影子斜。」小樹想盡辦法要讓堂姊擺脫負能量：「不要在意別人的看法或講法，有些人根本是外行充內行啊！如果你隨時都在意別人的質疑，那真的會在意不完的！」

曉梅沉默了一會兒，若有所思。

這時小樹靈光一現，想了個好點子，「與其困在家

melancholic, how about we go out to do something new?"

That was enough to pique Xiaomei's curiosity. "What do you have in mind, Xiaoshu?"

intrigued and asked curiously, "Do you have any suggestions?"

"Our uncle number 4, who serves in a non-profit organization, and the volunteer team leader Wu both introduced me to Ms. Huimei. That indicated that she is an expert in making presentations and organizing information. She may have a lot of stories to share, so let me see if we can have a chat with her," Xiaoshu said. Xiaoshu switched to his messaging function to text Mr. Huimei. Soon Xiaoshu said, "Great, she is free this afternoon. Let's go to her house."

Xiaomei was a little unsure about it, so Xiaoshu egged her on: "We can learn and explore through different ways, and we can also learn from others' experience." Xiaomei decided to go along.

After the two of them met up, they set out. Xiaoshu said, "Huimei has been a volunteer for 20 years, and she has compiled detailed information about the cases that she has been involved with, whether it is photos, texts, or audio-visual files. She has all of them carefully documented."

裡難過，我們要不要一起出門找點新鮮事？」

曉梅被勾起興趣，好奇地問：「你有什麼建議？」

「在公益團體服務的四叔還有志工吳小隊長，都不約而同跟我介紹過一位惠美阿姨，説她很會建檔做簡報、整理資料，她應該有很多故事可以分享，我來約約看。」小樹邊用電腦跟堂姊視訊，邊用手機簡訊跟惠美阿姨聯絡，「太好了，惠美阿姨下午有空，我們一起去她家吧。」

看出曉梅有一點點遲疑，小樹鼓勵説：「我們可以透過各種嘗試來學習探索，也可以經由別人的分享吸取經驗，或許原本心中的滯礙糾纏，可以獲得改善也不一定喔。」跟曉梅會合後，小樹在路上先簡單介紹惠美阿姨的背景。

「惠美阿姨當志工已經有二十年，她把二十年來陪伴個案的資料整理得很齊全，不論是照片、文字資料或影音檔，全都仔仔細細地建好檔了。」

"I admire volunteers, but I can't do it until I have the money and time," Xiaomei said in a low voice.

"Then you're in for a real surprise. Huimei is in poor health and her family is middle class. She once told us that volunteering is not reserved only for those who have money and leisure, but for anyone who is willing to serve others together." Before they knew it, they had reached Huimei's house.

"You must be Xiaoshu's cousin, Xiaomei. Welcome to my house. Xiaoshu, please help Xiaomei get comfortable. There are cut fruits and snacks on the table, and fruit tea," Huimei greeted her and Xiaoshu warmly, and then took them to sit down, turned on her laptop, and began to explain.

"This case is a story of skip-generation parenting. Both parents of these three cute children had died, so their grandma worked very hard to raise them in her home, which was very inaccessible. They had to travel to the city–a major undertaking–if the children needed to buy stationery and school supplies. Therefore, every pencil was used until it was too short for their little hands to hold. You can see from this photo that the three children were tightly holding their short pencils, which they cherished very much. The next photo

「我很佩服志工，可是這要等我有錢有閒時才能投入啦！」曉梅低聲回應。

「哪有這回事！惠美阿姨身體不好，家境也是小康而已，她就跟我們分享過：志工不是有錢有閒的人才能做，而是歡迎有心的人一起做！」小樹微笑說著。兩人不知不覺也到了惠美阿姨家門口。

「你就是小樹的堂姊曉梅吧，歡迎你。小樹，請幫忙招呼一下堂姊，餐桌上有切好的水果跟點心，還有水果茶。」惠美阿姨非常陽光熱情地打招呼，接著帶小樹跟曉梅入座後，打開筆電，開始溫柔地說明。

「這個案例是隔代教養的故事，這三個小孩都非常可愛，因為父母雙亡，所以由阿媽辛苦帶大三名孫子女。小時候因為阿媽家交通不便，買文具都還得搭車到市區才能買到，非常不容易，所以鉛筆常常用到短短禿禿的還捨不得丟。從這張照片可以看出來，三個孩子小小的手指緊緊握住短鉛筆，非常珍惜。接下來的照片是他們

shows their home as it was. Two discarded elementary school desks placed side by side formed their makeshift desk, where the three children huddled together to read, write, study, and do their homework. Their dining table was made up of several cardboard boxes glued together. Although they lived in a remote and humble place, these three children took their studies and homework very seriously. It was a happy family," Meihui said. Meihui's PowerPoint moved Xiaomei very much. She was in tears.

"I've always felt that children who know to cherish and appreciate will not go astray, and they will definitely do well for themselves," Xiaoshu said."Actually, there was not much that our volunteers could do for their family. We just occasionally helped them clean up their house inside and out, tidy up the house, repair the house, find some good second-hand furniture for them, and help them apply for living and education subsidies," Huimei added with a warm smile, "There was a small stationery store at the entrance to our alley, so before I visited them, I bought some notebooks, pencils, and erasers for them. That made them very happy, and I was very happy to see them happy."

家原來的樣子，這張小小舊舊由兩張廢棄小學課桌椅拼起來的，就是他們的克難書桌，三個小孩擠在一起讀書寫功課。這張用幾個紙箱黏在一起的，就是跟阿媽一起吃飯的餐桌。雖然他們住的地方很偏僻也很簡陋，可是這三個孩子做功課時很認真也很快樂。」看著簡報，聽惠美阿姨分享，曉梅很受感動，眼眶有點泛淚。

「我總覺得懂得珍惜與感謝的小孩不會變壞，一定有出息。」小樹感嘆。「其實我們志工能做的事也不多，只是偶爾幫忙打掃環境、整理家裡、修理房子，給他們找到一些好用的二手家具，還有幫他們申請生活與教育補助。」惠美暖暖地笑著補充，「我們家在巷口開了間小小文具店，去探望他們時，我會帶些筆記簿跟鉛筆、橡皮擦給他們，他們收到都好開心！看到他們開心，我也很高興。」

Xiaomei said, "This seemed to be a case of many years ago. I suppose these three children are grown up now."

To Xiaoshu, the three children in the photos did not appear sad, but instead they exuded warm energy, so he said, "They should change from knowing how to thank others for their help to being able to help others!"

Meihui pointed to the then and now photos of the children in the slide, and she couldn't stop smiling. The photo on the left was of three innocent children, and on the right was of three young and vigorous young people, "In 20 years, one of the children has gone from being a student to a teacher and returning to his alma mater to teach. Another child went from not being able to eat candy to becoming a convenience store manager, and the third child has gone from being shy and introverted to being a helpful policewoman. I'm absolutely thrilled; it's like seeing my own children grow up. These three children have gone from being aid recipients to aid givers."

"They're really three sensible and caring boys!" Xiaomei, seeming to have caught Meihui's energy, couldn't help but smile with relief.

"This kind of growth and maturity is more precious than success of any type," Xiaoshu said.

曉梅關心地問：「這個案例應該有好多年了，三個孩子現在都很大了吧？」

小樹感應到照片裡的孩子不但沒有愁容，還散發著溫暖的能量，「他們應該從懂得感謝別人的幫助，轉變為有能力幫助人的人了！」

惠美指著簡報裡，孩子們今昔的對比照片，笑容燦爛如花。左邊是三個天真無邪的小小孩、右邊是三個青春蓬勃年輕人的合影，「二十年，一個孩子從當學生變成老師回母校教書；一個孩子從吃不到糖果變成便利商店店長；一個孩子由害羞內向變成熱心助人的女警。好開心啊，就像看到自己的孩子孫女長大了一樣！這三個孩子都從手心向上、受人幫助，變成手心向下、幫助人的人了！」

「真的是三個懂事又有愛心的好孩子！」曉梅好像感染了惠美的能量與熱力一般，情不自禁的展開欣慰的笑容。

「這種長大成熟的結果比起任何的功成名就，更珍貴！」小樹也感觸良多。

Meihui opened another PowerPoint file.

"This is another case, and the photo shows Mr. Zhao, who was originally quite a headache in the neighborhood. He was single, unemployed, and an alcoholic. Every time he got drunk, he yelled at people and went crazy, and he threatened others with a fruit knife. The neighbors kept their doors shut for fear that he would come to the door to make trouble or, worse, hurt people."

"I was very worried when his case was assigned to me. I visited him only when I was accompanied by the neighborhood chief, the head of the HOA, or even the local police," Xiaomei said, shaking her head.

"Sometimes even the neighborhood chief is afraid of people like Mr. Zhao," Xiaoshu said with a wry smile.

"A few times a drunken Mr. Zhao took a taxi, but instead of going back to his own home directly, he got out of the taxi at the neighborhood chief's house and then demanded the chief pay the taxi driver. The chief agreed because he thought the fare would not amount to much and it would be futile for him to reason with a drunk. But he was shocked to find that the fare was more than NT$700. He was mad," Meihui said, trying to convey his facial expression.

分享完個案，惠美開啟另一個簡報檔。

「這是另一個個案，照片裡的是趙大哥，他原本是鄰里間相當讓人頭痛的人物：單身、無業又酗酒。每次喝醉了就會大吼大叫發酒瘋，還會拿水果刀威脅別人。以前左鄰右舍連門都不敢開，就怕他上門鬧事，更怕稍有不慎會遭傷害。」

「遇到這種個案真的很頭痛，我都要跟鄰里長、管委甚至當地員警一起上門。」曉梅搖搖頭。

「有時候鄰里長也很怕遇到這樣子的人吧！」小樹苦笑。

「里長遇到幾次趙大哥喝醉酒搭計程車，不直接回自己家，而是搭去里長家，然後指名要里長付錢。里長想說沒多少錢，跟醉酒的人爭論也是有理說不清，只好勉為其難答應了。結果一問，才驚覺車資竟然高達七百多元，氣到說不出話來。」惠美傳達著里長當時氣憤又無奈的表情。

"More than NT$700! That's pricey. Too bad for the chief," Xiaoshu said.

Shaking her head in disbelief, Xiaomei said after a while, "Is there a way to change such a troublesome character?"

"Everyone has their own characteristics and expertise, so we must observe closely. The first time we went to his house, I found that his bathroom and kitchen were immaculate; his pots and pans were neatly put away. Even old newspapers were perfectly and carefully stacked. I found him to have a ton of strengths, and I felt that he could be taught and changed."

"Despite all the bad things that everyone had said about this man, Huimei still tried to see the good in him," Xiaoshu nodded in agreement.

"Well, observe mindfully and find the good in others." Xiaomei jotted down the main points.

"I noticed that he often had soreness in his knees, so I gave him my medicine cloth to alleviate his discomfort," Meihui said, "I knew that he would do anything for a friend, so I planned a series of activities to help him quit drinking. If he had too much time on his hands, I was afraid that he would just drink to pass the time, so I arranged for him to volunteer at a recycling station and a local community center," Meihui

「七百多塊，好貴，里長虧大了！」小樹苦笑。

曉梅則是搖搖頭，隔了好一陣子才追問：「這樣讓人頭痛的麻煩人物，有辦法讓他改變嗎？」

「每個人都有自己的特色與專長，一定要仔細用心觀察。我們第一次去他家，發現他浴室、廚房都打理收拾得很乾淨，鍋碗瓢盆很整潔，尤其舊報紙更是四角對齊、仔細疊放。我發現他本身有很多優點，感覺可以教、可以被改變。」

「即使大家都說他是讓人頭痛的人物，但惠美阿姨仍努力看到他的優點。」小樹點頭深表認同。

「嗯，要仔細用心觀察，找出別人的優點。」曉梅記下重點。

「我發現他膝蓋不太好，常會痠痛，就拿家裡買的藥布給他貼，減輕他的不舒服。」惠美慢慢說明，「我了解他個性很講義氣，就計畫性地陸續安排，希望幫助他戒酒。因為怕他空閒時間太多，沒事做就想喝酒，所以介紹他去環保站幫忙資源回收，或去當地社區活動中

said, pointing to photos on the PowerPoint slides.

"He loved to be clean and was quite an expert in keeping things very tidy, so he really shined at the recycling station, very nicely tidying up messy recyclables and tools. And because he had become a volunteer at the community center, his relationship with the neighbors also improved. Someone referred him to work the night shift as a security guard in a warehouse, and before long he made the entire warehouse really neat and orderly. He also swept and cleaned the plant and set up a recycling station there. His boss was very happy with him and gave him a raise."

"Keep him busy doing things, and he won't be so bored as to bother other people," Xiaoshu found the whole thing intriguing. Not only had Mr. Zhao stopped drinking, but he had transformed himself from being feared to being loved by everyone.

"That's a great way to channel his expertise into a catalyst for change!" Xiaomei thought highly of Huimei's approach.

Huimei was committed to and happily doing what she was doing. Xiaomei was lost in thought. She admired and envied Huimei from the bottom of her heart.

心當義工。」惠美一邊指著簡報的檔案照片，一邊說明。「他愛乾淨、又擅長把東西整理得非常整齊，在環保站果然大展身手，把雜亂的資源回收物跟工具整理得井然有序。又因為當了社區活動中心的義工，跟鄰里之間的關係也改善了，還有人主動介紹他做工廠倉庫夜間警衛的工作，結果真的把倉庫管理得非常整潔有序，還主動打掃廠房，也設了資源回收點，老闆很高興、還給他加薪呢！」

「讓他忙著動手做事，就不會無聊到動手傷人了！」小樹覺得很有意思，也感應到趙大哥由人見人怕到人見人愛的變化。

「讓他的專長變成改變的動力，這個方式很不錯！」曉梅覺得惠美阿姨的做法可以參考。

聽到這，曉梅有點發愣，陷入自己的思緒裡。她發自內心羨慕惠美阿姨：能夠這麼投入這麼快樂，真好！

Xiaoshu said to Xiaomei, "The story is wonderful, but don't forget the fruit and snacks."

Meihui smiled and said, "Yes, please have some snacks and allow me to tell the story of a new resident and her sister-in-law."

Meihui opened the last PowerPoint file and pointed to the first photo of the two women, "Don't they look like best friends in this photo? They used to live in the same house, one on the upstairs and the other downstairs, but they hated each other's guts," Huimei said. "The sister-in-law lived on the first floor, and the new resident and her family lived on the second floor. The main shutoff valve of water is located on the first floor. Because the bathroom on the second floor was a little leaky, the sister-in-law often turned off the valve, arguing that the leakage would lead to higher water bills and totally ignoring the fact that it would also deprive the family on the second floor of water. Under the watchful eyes of her sister-in-law, the new resident had to go to a local temple or park to get water and carry it home, which is very troublesome. It stands to reason, then, that the two families did not eat at the same table."

"The two of them despised each other so much that each time they came face to face, they would without fail exchange

小樹見狀提醒堂姊：「故事很好聽，水果點心也別忘了捧場，是惠美阿姨用心準備的。」

　　惠美笑笑說：「對對對，一邊吃一邊再聽我講新住民外配跟她單身大姑的故事。」

　　惠美打開最後一個簡報檔，指著第一張兩個女人的合照，「你們別看這張照片裡兩位像閨密一樣，以前她們住樓上樓下，卻是王不見王、水火不容。」惠美強調：「大姑住一樓，弟媳一家住二樓。自來水的總開關在一樓，因為二樓浴室有點漏水，大姑就常常關總開關，不讓弟媳一家用水，說漏水會增加水電費。在大姑的管控下，弟媳還要去土地公廟跟公園打水提水，很麻煩，吃飯也是兩家分開，各自開伙。」

　　「她們兩個人以前對對方都很有怨念，每次見面一

noisy verbal attacks," Xiaoshu could imagine how much it must be like the tit for tat in soap operas.

"The issues between mother-in-laws and daughter-in-laws or between in-laws are often next to impossible to solve," Xiaoshu believed that Xiaomei had seen plenty of replays in other cases.

"The sister-in-law would complain about the new resident—her own brother's wife–to anyone who would listen: "She speaks to me in rude language, and she has a very bad attitude. She speaks with her hands resting on her waist. If she doesn't respect me as her elder, why should I take care of her?"

Meihui said that she could see where either party was coming from. "The new resident was also helpless, and she would also complain about her sister-in-law to anyone who would listen. She said that it was customary for people in her hometown to talk with their hands on their waists, and people there were all straight shooters. They did not mince their words. Talking the way she did was nothing out of the ordinary in her hometown. She meant no malice. She complained that her sister-in-law was too sensitive and, by turning off the main shutoff valve, caused great inconvenience to her family. She asked why she should respect her sister-in-law."

定吵得很熱鬧！」小樹可以想像這兩個女人過去跟演八點檔連續劇一樣，針鋒相對。

「婆媳之間或姑嫂妯娌的問題，往往都是難解的題目！」相關的抱怨，相信曉梅已從以往個案處聽過不少。

「大姑見人就唸：弟媳態度很差，一見面就凶巴巴地兩手叉腰一直罵人，好像母老虎，沒禮貌，怎麼會有這種人？我是大姑，也算是長輩，一點長幼有序的觀念都沒有！不把我當長輩，我為什麼要顧到她？」

惠美形容大姑跟弟媳兩邊都各有立場，「弟媳這邊也很無奈，見人就訴苦：手叉腰講話是家鄉習慣，那裡人人都是直腸子，這樣對話很平常，又沒有惡意！她自己想太多還怪我？害我們用水這麼不方便，我為什麼要尊敬她？」

"That's quite vexing. How did Huimei bring the two of them together?" Xiaoshu said, shaking his head, "This kind of situation where everyone seems to have a point is a tough nut to crack."

"But Huimei must have a way!" Xiaomei was quite sure.

"I suggested to the new resident, who worked in a restaurant of a hotel and had a habit of packing leftover food for her husband and son, to divide the leftover into two parts and give one part to her sister-in-law as a gesture of goodwill. After doing this a few times, I believe that the sister-in-law would definitely feel respected. I also suggested that she sugarcoat her words a little so that her sister-in-law would be happier."

"When she flattered her sister-in-law, if her tone and attitude remained cold or if she talked with her hands on her hips as she had always done, then I'd say her sister-in-law would probably not be impressed," Xiaoshu said.

"That's right! I asked the new resident's husband to video record a phone conversation between his wife and me. I also explained to her that the customs about talking varied by location. In Taiwan, if we talk with our hands on our waists, that means we are angry. That's why her sister-in-law had been feeling bad, and I suggested that she should change her habit.

「傷腦筋！惠美阿姨怎麼解開她們兩位的心結呢？」小樹搖頭，「這種姑說姑有理、媳說媳有理的狀況感覺很難處理！」

「惠美阿姨一定有辦法！」曉梅很有信心。

「我就教在飯店餐廳打工的弟媳，把每次為先生和兒子打包的剩菜分成兩份，多的一份就送給大姑，以表示善意。這樣幾次以後，相信大姑一定會改變，覺得被尊重了。還有，嘴巴可以甜一點，要常喊大姑好，這樣她一定更開心。」

「光是嘴巴甜，但語氣態度還是很兇，加上還手叉著腰講話，恐怕效果會打折扣喔！」小樹想想覺得好笑。

「沒錯！我跟弟媳的先生講，請他在我跟他老婆對話時，在一旁用手機錄影。也跟弟媳說明各地風俗民情不同，在我們這裡兩手叉腰講話像似在生氣罵人，難怪大姑會感覺不舒服，建議她最好改過來。同時也讓弟媳

At the same time, I also asked her to watch the video to see the difference between talking with and without putting hands on the waist. Now she smiles when she meets people, and she doesn't talk with her hands on her waist anymore."

"After she had extended the olive branch, I'd think that her sister-in-law would change, too," Xiaomei asked.

"As the new resident kept extending her goodwill, her sister-in-law was embarrassed. One day when our volunteers were helping their family repair their water pipes, she asked them to extend one more water pipe upstairs so that her brother's family could have access to water." Xiaoshu and Xiaomei heaved a collective sigh of relief. Meihui continued, "In the past, the meal time and living space of the two families did not mix and were strictly separated, but now they eat together and they share their home space," Huimei said."That's great. Respecting and loving each other, that is a family!" Xiaoshu was very happy about this happy ending.

When they left Huimei's house, Xiaoshu and Xiaomei felt that they had learned a lot. Looking at Xiaomei in the eyes, Huimei said to her, "Choose what you love, and love the job you choose. Listen to your own heart, use your heart to help the needy, and God will take care of you."

自己看手機錄影，看看手叉腰跟不叉腰的差別。現在弟媳遇到人都會笑咪咪，也不再兩手叉腰說話了。」

「大姑這邊接收到弟媳先釋出的善意，應該也會跟著改變吧！」曉梅問。

「當弟媳愈來愈親切有禮，大姑自然不好意思了！在我們志工幫她們家修水管時，她也主動提出，再多牽一條水管接到樓上，讓弟媳一家方便用水。」惠美看著小樹跟曉梅同時鬆了一口氣的神情，強調：「以前兩家是各吃各的飯，樓上樓下壁壘分明；現在兩家是一家人，餐食分享、空間共享呢！」

「太好了，彼此尊重互相友愛，這才是一家人！」小樹很滿意這個快樂的結局。

臨離開惠美阿姨家時，小樹跟曉梅都覺得自己收穫好多。惠美阿姨仔細地看了看曉梅後，輕聲地提醒：「選擇自己愛的，也愛自己選擇的工作！用心傾聽自己的心，用心幫助他們，老天也會來眷顧妳的。」

Turning to look at Xiaomei, feeling the light and warm energy flowing between Huimei, Xiaomei, and himself, Xiaoshu said with relief, "You yourself know best if it is worth it. Do your job the best you can. We're all our best cheerleaders. Come on! Let's go!"

小樹轉頭看向曉梅，感受著在惠美阿姨、曉梅堂姊與自己之間流動的光與溫暖的能量，欣慰地說：「值不值得自己最知道！做好自己的工作，我們都是自己最好的啦啦隊，加油！」

The Magic of A Postive Attitude

Positive self-talk when you feel low:
I can do it, I've done it very well.
Mindfulness Practice:
Stay calm and focused, reduce stress, and enhance self-affirmation.
Look for support systems around you:
Talk to positive, supportive friends and family.
Accept criticism:
Treat other people's opinions as an opportunity to learn and grow.
Enhance your sense of self-worth:
Constantly learning new skills or interests to enrich
your personal life.
Through these methods you become your own cheerleader and you
are motivated to keep moving forward.

正能量的磁場效應

低潮時積極自我對話：

我可以做到，我已經做得很好

正念練習：

保持冷靜和專注，減少壓力，增強自我肯定

尋找周圍支持系統：

與積極、支持你的朋友和家人交流

接受批評：

把別人的觀點當作是學習和成長的機會

增強自我價值感：

不斷學習新技能或興趣，充實個人生活

通過這些方法，成為自己的啦啦隊，激勵持續前進

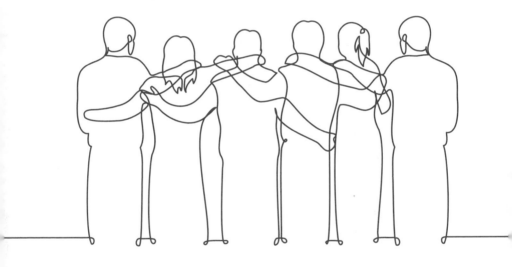

第六章
CHAPTER 6

柳暗花明的轉角

Surprises after the river bend

When the class was over and everyone rushed out, Xiaoshu said to a classmate, "Zhixiang, any thoughts on the 'People and Things' group report that the teacher assigned us to do?"

Zhixiang shrugged and said, "I don't have any ideas yet. We'll cross the bridge when we come to it, I guess. If worse comes to worst, we can always just ask AI chatbots. Do you have any good ideas?"

Xiaoshu thought for a moment, and slowly explained as he walked, "I mentioned our group report when I was chatting with a few cousins online a few days ago, and they all liked our teacher's idea of that assignment. They said that gossipping was all the rage and negative energy abounded on the net. Many people, hiding under the protective umbrella of the Internet, turn their keyboards into a weapon of massive disinformation, slander, cynicism, ridiculing, or vicious personal attacks. Few people are interested in unearthing and sharing heart-warming stories around them any more."

Zhixiang nodded in agreement as Xiaoshu continued, "People are too easily believing what they see or hear on the net. They do not verify, and there is too much acerbic language out there that's not responsible and outright false."

Zhixiang said, "You mean, it's best not to believe

放學時，小樹伸手攔住正急急忙忙準備回家的同學知翔。

　　「知翔，老師説的『這些人那些事』小組故事報告，你有想法了嗎？」

　　知翔兩手一攤聳聳肩説：「還沒有任何想法！反正船到橋頭自然直，就網路上找找題材好了。你有什麼好建議嗎？」

　　小樹思索了一下，邊走邊慢慢説明：「前幾天我跟幾位堂表兄弟姊妹在網路社群上聊天時，有提到我們這個小組報告題目，他們都很喜歡老師規定的這個作業。大家都説現在八卦當道，網路上總有許多負能量！很多人隱藏在網路這個保護傘下，搖身一變為鍵盤酸民，奚落訕笑甚至惡毒批評乃至落井下石者不可勝數，反而很少有人熱衷去挖掘身邊溫馨的故事。」

　　知翔認同地點點頭，小樹接著補充：「而且網路上大家容易看到什麼就相信什麼，也不會認真仔細去求證，不負責任的留言評論或酸言苛語都很多。」

　　知翔聞言提問：「你的意思是，最好不要光看單方

unilateralstatements, but best to verify it?"

Xiaoshu smiled and nodded, "That's right! Just like I've read on the Internet about a very special restaurant, and even though I feel that it may be suitable for our 'People and Things' presentation, we must pay the place a visit to ensure that it actually does meet our requirements."

Xiaoshu said as he turned to look at Zhixiang, "Are you free this Saturday? Do you want to go with me? I've already made an appointment to meet with the main subject in that store during a slow period."

Zhixiang stopped in surprise and said, "Xiaoshu, you're moving in overdrive! Of course I'm going. We're in the same group, and if I go, I can help take pictures and record the interview." Then he said a little hesitantly, "But, is it expensive?"

"Don't worry; the shop is very affordable! My eldest cousin is a regular customer, and he said that he would join us that day and it would be his treat."

"Okay, definitely count me in," Zhixiang said.

The weather on Saturday could not be better, with blue skies and white clouds and a gentle cool breeze. Zigzagging through the winding streets, Xiaoshu and Zhixiang had a feeling of going on a hike together.

面説法，應該要多方去實地求證？」

小樹微笑説明：「沒錯！就像網路上有人說有一家很特別的餐飲店，我看網路上面講的那家店的故事，感覺還滿適合我們『這些人那些事』的報告題材，但我們還是必須去實際走訪，親自去查證清楚，看看這個題材是不是符合我們作業報告的要求。」

小樹轉頭看著知翔：「這個星期六你有沒有空？要不要一起去？主要的採訪對象我已經約好了。地點就約在那家店裡，時間請店家安排在比較空閒、顧客比較少的空檔。」

知翔驚訝地停下腳步，讚嘆道：「小樹，你動作也太快了吧！我當然要參加，我們可是同一組的，我去的話，還可以幫忙拍照、錄音喔。」接著有點遲疑地問：「可是……那間店的消費會不會很貴？」

「不用擔心，那家店的消費很平價啦！我大表哥是常客，他説那天他當陪客，他要請客喔。」

「好，我一定會去！」知翔肯定地答應。

星期六天氣大好，藍天白雲還有徐徐涼風，穿梭在彎彎拐拐的街道裡，小樹和知翔有種結伴郊遊的感覺。

"If you didn't take me here, I wouldn't know that there is such a small, garden-like restaurant hiding in the alleys."

Various plants on the clear windowsill and the flowers and plants neatly surrounding the gate, Zhixiang exclaimed, "This is really a paradise hidden in the street!" He couldn't stop taking pictures everywhere.

"This place is a well-kept secret, where people may soak up the healing effect of plants," Xiaoshu said as he stood at the door and took deep breaths, feeling endless energy streaming into himself. "This is very much like an oasis in the desert, giving the soul a good place to rest, breathe, and recharge."

Xiaoshu turned to look at a small potted plant by the door, and suddenly he had a strange sensation of a powerful message coming along the cool and sweet mint smell towards him.

Zhixiang nodded and said, "The name of the store is 'The Bend'. How romantic! Its proprietor may as well be a big fan of idol dramas, like 'The Next Stop Named Happiness', 'Meet Love Around the Corner', and the like. Perhaps dating at this restaurant could go smoother in such an environment." When taking pictures, Zhixiang made sure that he captured the restaurant's small wooden signs that were scattered everywhere.

「你不說我還不知道，老街巷弄裡竟然還有這麼一間森林系的小餐館。」

看著眼前透明窗檯上各式各樣的植栽，大門四周還環繞別緻的花花草草，知翔一邊讚嘆：「這真是隱藏在街道裡的世外桃源！」一邊忍不住朝不同角落拍照。

「這是城市裡的祕境，讓人有機會跟植物來場療癒的約會。」小樹站在門口深呼吸，感應著源源不絕的能量往自己集中，「這裡很像是沙漠裡的綠洲，給心靈一個休憩、喘息、充電的好地方。」

小樹轉頭看向門邊一個小盆栽，忽然有種奇怪的感應，好像有什麼強而有力的訊息，順著清涼香甜的薄荷味傳遞過來。

知翔點點頭說：「真浪漫，店名叫『轉角』！老闆應該是偶像劇的忠實粉絲，像《下一站幸福》、《轉角遇到愛》之類的，在這樣的環境氛圍裡約會談戀愛，應該會比較順利喔。」拍照時，知翔不忘讓各處小小的木製店招入鏡。

Xiaoshu stood in front of the floor-to-ceiling display at the entrance of the store, concentrating on studying the calligraphy words on it: Just as the mountain and the river seem to block all paths forward, dark willows become bright, flowers and a new village reveals itself in front of your eyes. Xiaoshu said to himself, "I think the name of the store 'The Bend' means something deep."

Before entering the door, Xiaoshu couldn't help but look at the small potted plant by the door, which was a particularly dense mint, and at this time there seemed to be a faint soft music lingering in his ears.Xiaoshu wondered if this little potted plant had something to say to him. Without thinking about it, he crouched down and whispered to the pot of mint, "What's the special story about you? Among this group of potted plants here, you seem to be a little different." Of course, the pot of mint was silent. Zhixiang turned around and lightly called Xiaoshu to proceed, and Xiaoshu hurriedly got up and walked into the store.

After entering the store and taking their seats, Xiaoshu and Zhixiang spread out essential items for an interview: the voice recorder on the table along with the camera, interview consent form, and so forth.

小樹站在店門口落地展示架前，專心研究著上面的書法字：山窮水盡疑無路，柳暗花明又一村，「我覺得『轉角』這個店名，應該還有別的意思吧。」

　　進門前，小樹忍不住定睛細看門邊的小盆栽，是一株長得特別茂密的薄荷，這時耳邊似乎隱約縈繞著輕柔的樂音。小樹不免疑惑，難道這個小盆栽有什麼話要跟我說嗎？他沒有細想就蹲下對這盆薄荷輕聲說：「你身上有什麼奇特的故事呢？在身邊一群各色各樣的小盆栽裡，你好像有點不太一樣呢。」當然，薄荷寂然無語，知翔轉身輕喚小樹，小樹就趕忙起身走進店門了。

　　進到店裡入座後，小樹和知翔把錄音筆跟相機、受訪同意書等等一一攤放在桌上。

Zhixiang looked around and asked, "In addition to the fact that there are a lot of flowers and plants in this shop, and the layout is very elegant, there must be something else that makes it special."

"I heard that in the winter, the store will serve hot sweet potato and ginger soup for free for everyone who comes to the store, and in the summer, it will serve a refreshing mint lemon sparkling drink. Customers can drink them to their hearts' content." Xiaoshu said.

"No kidding. That's a money-losing proposition for restaurants. This way of hospitality doesn't seem businesssmart. If customers can get something free, they won't spend money buying it." Zhixiang shook his head in disapproval.

"People also say that the most special thing about this restaurant is that there are occasional lucky meals and good luck dim sum that only very few customers will get, and they are also free, of course," Xiaoshu whispered.

"Is this some sort of membership point collection scheme, or only those who meet sky-high threshold have a shot at those freebies?" Zhixiang's eyes widened and he had a renewed respect for the proprietor. "The owner does have a way of running his business," he continued.

知翔朝四周看了一下，好奇發問：「這間店除了有很多花花草草、布置很幽雅以外，應該還有一些特別的地方吧！」

　　「聽説店家在冬天的時候會供應熱騰騰的地瓜薑湯，讓來店的人免費取用，夏天則是清涼薄荷檸檬氣泡飲，都是不限量的。」小樹説道。

　　「真的假的？餐飲店這樣做會虧本的，這種招待的方式太不聰明了！有免費的，大家就不會多花錢消費了。」知翔搖頭，十分不以為然。

　　「還有一種説法，這間店最特別的是：偶爾會出現很少人有機會吃得到的幸運餐和好運點心，也是免費的。」小樹低聲説。

　　「該不會要集點辦會員，那種設了高門檻才能到手的超級貴賓級好禮？」知翔睜大眼，改變自己對老闆的評價，「老闆做生意有一套！」

"No. I heard that those freebies are given out randomly, and only those who are destined to have them can get them. This will make those winners very happy, change their lives, and bring them good luck." Xiaoshu smiled.

"So mysterious! I'll have to ask them later to find out what the heck is going on?" Zhixiang was gearing up, and he couldn't wait."

The proprietor is somewhat low-key, and it is not easy for us to get his consent to our visit today," Xiaoshu whispered, "However, he will arrive later, and the first person to talk to us will be Mr. Zhao, who had won a lucky meal."

"Wow, you even made an appointment for this?" Zhixiang looked at Xiaoshu in disbelief, and Xiaoshu nodded slightly.

As soon as they finished talking, someone approached their table.

"Excuse me, are you Xiaoshu and Zhixiang? Hello." A gentleman greeted them with a smile and handed over his business card, "My last name is Zhao, but I go by Wenzhan."

Xiaoshu carefully observed Mr. Zhao and sensed his confidence and cheerfulness.

After Mr. Zhao signed the consent form for the interview, Xiaoshu went directly to the topic: "Wenzhang, under what

「不是喔，聽説老闆是隨機的，有緣人才吃得到。吃到的人非常高興，生活上也會發生變化，帶來好運。」小樹微笑。

「這麼神祕！待會一定要好好問問，這到底是怎麼回事？」知翔摩拳擦掌、迫不及待。

「老闆是一個有點低調的人，這次是好不容易才答應我們的訪問。」小樹低聲説，「不過，老闆要晚點才來，待會先到的是一位吃過幸運餐的趙先生。」

「哇，你連這個都約好了？」知翔不敢置信地看向小樹，小樹輕輕點頭。

話剛説完，就有人向他們的座位走來。

「請問是小樹同學跟知翔同學嗎？你們好。」一位溫文有禮的男子微笑打招呼，邊遞來名片，「我姓趙，你們可以叫我文章哥。」

小樹仔細地觀察著趙先生，感應到他身上的自信與開朗。

請趙先生簽完受訪同意書之後，小樹直接進入主題：

circumstances did you come to "The Bend' to dine?" Zhixiang quickly pressed the recorder button.

"It's hard for you to believe that when I first walked into this shop, it was the darkest and most painful stage of my life, and I really thought I was at the end of my rope!

"My friend convinced me to invest in cryptocurrencies with him. I trusted him because we went back a long way. We were neighbors and good friends growing up together. So not only did I take out all my savings to support him, but I also mortgaged my house to increase my investment! But he vanished the moment he got my money. I've tried a lot of ways and used many channels, but he's nowhere to be seen."

Zhixiang looked surprised, and Xiaoshu expressed his deep sympathy, "We sympathize with your loss. To lose so much money was bad enough, but to be betrayed by a good friend made it all that much more difficult to bear."

Zhao Wenzhang sighed and continued, "Right. Though starting from scratch is exceedingly hard, the money that I lost can be made again. However, I was thoroughly disappointed by his betrayal and human nature, and I totally lost hope. It felt like I was falling into an abyss, unable to climb out again. I was walking down the road in a daze, like a zombie, and I didn't

「文章哥，你是在怎樣的情況下來到『轉角』用餐？可以請你描述一下當時的經過嗎？」知翔一旁迅速按下錄音筆。

　　「你們大概很難相信，當初走進這間店的時候，正是我人生最灰暗慘痛的階段，我當時真的以為我已經山窮水盡了！

　　「朋友說服我一起去投資虛擬貨幣，我很信任他，因為是從小一起長大的鄰居、更是好朋友。所以我不只把所有積蓄拿出來支持他，還拿自己的房子抵押增貸去加碼投資！

　　「沒想到，他拿到錢以後就從此消失！我試了很多方法、透過很多管道都找不到人！」

　　聽到這，知翔一臉驚訝，小樹則深表同情，「文章哥說的我們可以體會：金錢上的損失慘重已經很難過了，被好朋友詐騙跟背叛更是非常沉重的打擊。」

　　趙文章嘆了口氣，繼續說：「對，金錢失去了可以再賺，從零開始雖然很辛苦但也不是辦不到！可是真正傷我的是那種對人性的徹底失望，真的很絕望，就像掉入深淵，再也無力爬出來！

know why I walked into this shop. At that time, a terrible thought flashed in my mind: This might be my last meal, so I just ordered the menu item that my eyes happened to stare at. It wouldn't matter anyway!

"Surprisingly, a female store employee came over to my table and said excitedly, 'Congratulations! You are our lucky guest. Your lucky meal and good luck dim sum today are on the house.'

"I looked at her in disbelief and asked her wryly, 'What luck? Do you mean me? Believe me, nobody in the world had worse luck than me.

"The worker didn't seem to hear what I had said as she continued to enthusiastically introduce the lucky meal and good luck dim sum. She indicated how rare they were and how precious they were. From appetizers, soup, the main course, to the dessert. She also said that the ingredients of the meal had been carefully planted and harvested by her boss, the proprietor, who also carefully designed each dish. Anyway, the lucky meal is not available on the menu to ensure that those who are lucky enough to eat it get the highest enjoyment and energy possible.

"At that time, I had lost heart, so I just interrupted the

「當時我迷迷糊糊走在路上，整個人呆呆傻傻地像遊魂一樣，也不知道為什麼會走進這間店？

　　「當時心中甚至浮現一個可怕的念頭：這說不定是我人生的最後一餐了，就隨便點吧！反正無所謂了！

　　「很意外的，這時有一位女店員突然跑過來，用極興奮的語調對我說：『恭喜！您是我們的幸運貴賓，今天的幸運餐跟好運點心我們免費招待！』

　　「我不敢相信地看著她，苦笑地問：什麼幸運？你是說我嗎？相信我，全天下應該沒有比我更慘的人了！

　　「女店員似乎沒聽到我說了什麼，她繼續熱心不減地介紹幸運餐跟好運點心，說這有多難得、比限量品還要珍貴等等，從前菜、湯、主食到點心飲料，內容非常豐富。還說餐點的食材是老闆用心栽種、每道餐的內容也是老闆精心設計，是不會出現在菜單上的隱藏版，保證讓幸運吃到的人獲得滿滿的能量。

　　「當時我萬念俱灰，直接打斷女店員滔滔不絕的介

worker's gushing introduction and told her very firmly that I was not that hungry, that I had no appetite, and that please just give me a small helping–to save a lot of trouble for the chef.

"Incredulous, she looked a little at a loss. She muttered that it would be a great pity to squander such a great meal and great luck, that others couldn't get that meal even if they wanted to order it, that I'd be sorry if I missed this opportunity that only came once in a blue moon."

"It's a pity that you turned the good luck away," Xiaoshu said.

Zhao Wenzhang smiled and continued, "To be honest, I didn't want to make it hard for her to do her job, and she was really sincerely trying to help me, so I told her to go ahead and serve up the lucky meal and everything else that would come with it, but just give me a small serving and share the rest of the meal with all the guests in the restaurant.

"I watched the worker enthusiastically inform guests at other tables of what was to come. I couldn't be more downbeat at the time, and I certainly didn't believe that one meal, however lucky it might be, could possibly bring me luck. So, just leave me alone in my miserable abyss to be bypassed by any good luck."

紹，很堅定地跟她說我其實不太餓，沒什麼胃口、也吃不太下，請盡量簡單給我一小份就好，用不著那麼麻煩。

「女店員聽完就愣愣地看著我，顯得有點手足無措。她滿臉疑問，喃喃嘟嚷著：可惜！難得您有這麼好的運氣，這是相當難得的好機會呢，別人想吃都吃不到，錯過的話會很遺憾喔！」

小樹跟知翔聽到這，臉上也是不可置信的表情。「好運都到你面前了，居然還往外推，這未免太可惜了吧！」小樹說。

趙文章笑了一下，繼續說：「說實話，我也不想為難那位女店員，也覺得她說可惜時的態度非常真誠，所以我想了一下就說：不然就給我小小一盤主食加一點配菜就好，其他的，請你分給其他桌，請大家一起吃吧。

「我看著女店員走向其他桌，熱心地一一向客人們解釋。當時我心中仍然充滿了自棄的陰影：就把幸運分給其他人吧！我這麼倒楣，不需要一份餐點帶來的好運，還是讓我孤零零地待在黑暗深淵，默默地被好運所遺棄吧！」

Immersed in memories, Zhao continued, "Food was served for me shortly after: a small plate of scrambled eggs with tomato and steaming hot vegetable noodles. Perfectly presented, green beans, broccoli, carrots, baby mustard, and the mouth-watering aroma of basil accompanied the noodles. I took a bite and found it to be better than I expected. I found that all the ingredients were fresh and delicious, and I could just feel just how much the chef painstakingly attended to the dishes.

"Then I thought to myself that it was actually nice to be able to share the lucky meal with everyone in the restaurant. I couldn't finish it by myself anyway.

"I was going to remain quietly immersed in my own little world, but I couldn't because people kept interrupting me–to thank me."

Thank you! The chef had carefully attended to the sesame tofu. It's so delicious!

Thank you for sharing the lucky meal with me.

I feel like I have a lot of positive energy to share with others!

Handmade multigrain bread is special. I tasted red quinoa, and a wide variety of whole grains.

沉浸在回憶中，趙文章繼續說道：「分配好之後，不久就上菜了。就看到眼前一小盤冒著輕煙與熱氣的番茄炒蛋跟蔬菜麵。擺盤很用心，有青豆、綠花椰和紅蘿蔔、娃娃菜，還散發著一股好聞的九層塔香氣。」

　　「我當時吃了第一口，發現它比想像中來得好吃。我發覺所有的材料都很新鮮，味道也很鮮美，可以充分感受到烹調者的用心。

　　「當時我腦海裡閃過一個念頭：能夠把這個美味的幸運餐和好運點心分享出去，讓別人也能夠品嘗到，其實也滿不錯的。反正我一個人也吃不完。

　　「我本來想安靜地繼續沉浸在自己的世界，後來卻被一個又一個過來道謝的人打斷思緒。」

　　謝謝你！那道芝麻豆腐做得好用心。入口綿密，太好吃了！

　　謝謝你把幸運餐分給我。

　　我覺得我有滿滿正能量可以分享給別人了！

　　手工雜糧麵包很特別，我吃得到紅藜，和各式各樣的五穀雜糧。

Thank you for sharing, and I feel that you have shared your good luck with me, too.

That roselle nectar tea is delicious. T hank you.

You're an incredibly nice person to share your good luck with everyone.

I have never drunk such a delicious and nutritiousvegetable soup. And it is indeed a lucky meal, the soup is full of vitality as soon as you eat it!

My mom said that I couldn't accept other people's gif ts for nothing, and she asked me to come over here to thank you.

Lemon sea salt ice cream is the best.

Thank you. I want to give this to you—my favorite chocolate lollipop.

People, men and women, young and old, one after another, came to Wenzhang to thank him. Some of them said, "I stared at the lollipop in front of me with wide eyes, and I felt as if I had received the most valuable gift in the world."

"The Bend seemed to suddenly come alive, and I felt that I was the sun sitting in the middle, looking at the planets around me, smiling and greeting me, projecting warmth and kindness."whole restaurant.

Strange, isn't it? Zhao Wenzhang merely and mindlessly

感謝你的分享，我覺得也分享到你的好運呢！

那個洛神花蜜茶好好喝，謝謝你。

怎麼有這麼好的人，把好運分給大家共享？！

我沒喝過這麼美味又營養的蔬菜湯，果然是幸運餐，湯一入口，活力滿滿！

我媽說不能白拿別人的禮物，要我過來謝謝叔叔。

檸檬海鹽冰淇淋最好吃。

謝謝叔叔。這是我最喜歡吃的巧克力棒棒糖，分給你吃。

接二連三的，男男女女老老少少都跑來文章哥這裡道謝說感恩：「我睜大眼睛瞪著眼前的棒棒糖，感覺好像收到世界上最貴重的禮物。」

「這間『轉角』好像忽然轉動熱鬧了起來，我像是坐在中間的太陽，看著四周星球圍繞，向我微笑打招呼，投射著溫暖和善意。」

shared the lucky meal and the good luck dim sum, but he was thanked and rewarded with kindness from everyone in the whole restaurant.

"When I left The Bend, I no longer felt lonely and helpless, and I realized one thing: just because I met a bad friend who would cheat me out of my money didn't mean I'd never have a chance to meet a good friend. As long as I am willing to show kindness, I believe that there are still many upright, thoughtful, and sincere people in the world who are worthy of my friendship."

"Great! The blessing of Lucky Meal and Good Luck Dim Sum was not diluted because of sharing, but instead it was amplified," Xiaoshu felt the energy and warmth flowing in Zhao Wenzhang. Because of his sharing, he received everyone's feedback and gathered from their strength, which seemingly turned into a sturdy rope and a long ladder with which Zhao Wenzhang climbed out of his mental abyss and saw the bright sun.

It was Zhao Wenzhang who first showed friendliness to share, albeit inadvertently, which led others in the restaurant to give back to him, thus giving him strength to pick himself up from financial ruin.

很奇怪吧！趙文章只是隨意地把幸運餐和好運點心分享出去，卻得到了整間餐廳所有人充滿善意的感謝與回報。

　　「我離開『轉角』時，不再覺得自己孤獨無助，我明白一件事：不幸遇到一個會詐騙的壞朋友，不代表我從此就沒機會遇到好人！只要肯釋出善意，相信世界上還有很多值得交往、用心對待的人等著去認識。」

　　「太好了！幸運餐跟好運點心沒有因為分享而減少福氣，反而發揮了更強大的力量、互相吸引形成更大的磁場！」小樹感受著趙文章身上流動的能量與暖意，因為他的分享，反而得到大家回饋、進而匯聚眾人之力，化成結實的繩索與長梯，讓身處深淵的趙文章得以爬出谷底，看到了陽光。

　　是趙文章無意間先表現出友善與分享，讓眾人可以回饋，也投射力量助他一臂之力！

Catching a hint from Xiaoshu, Zhixiang quickly snapped his camera, just in time to capture the moments when Zhao Wenzhang was smiling with emotion and tears were swirling in his eyes.

After Zhao Wenzhang left, Zhixiang said to Xiaoshu, "This lucky meal and good luck dim sum really have a mysterious power!"

Xiaoshu pondered, nodded and said, "I think energy is indestructible and will go around. The kindness extended by Wenzhang made a full circle and went back to himself in a wonderful way, and the real luck and good fortune actually came from the choices he unintentionally made."

Zhixiang nodded, but he didn't really understand: "The proprietor must be very rich, and it is very likely that he was born into a rich family. He wants to give back to society with this mysterious surprise and see everyone's reaction."

"Hold that thought, and you can ask the proprietor yourself."

Just then, a woman, her clothing suggesting a chef, about 30 years old, slowly came out of the kitchen. She removed the clear mask from her face, took off her apron and gloves, and, with a smile, walked towards them.

知翔笑著點頭接住了小樹的暗示，迅速敏捷地用相機捕捉到：趙文章眼眶裡打轉的淚光，閃過一抹充滿感動與溫暖的笑意。

趙文章離開後，知翔跟小樹說：「這個幸運餐跟好運點心真的有種神祕的力量耶！」

小樹思索著，點頭慎重地說：「我覺得能量是不滅的，是會循環的。文章哥拋出去的善意，用很棒的方式回到他自己身上，真正的幸運與好運其實是來自無意之間他做的選擇！」

知翔似懂非懂地點點頭：「老闆一定很有錢，很有可能是富二代。所以想藉著這個神祕驚喜來回饋社會，順便看看大家的反應。」

「等一下你可以自己問老闆。」

就在此刻，從廚房裡緩緩走出一個穿戴得像專業廚師，約莫三十多歲的女性。她取下臉上的透明口罩、脫掉圍裙和手套，微笑著朝他們走來。

"Hello, Xiaoshu and Zhixiang? I'm between tasks in the kitchen, so I can talk to you while I'm free. I am Lu Xinyi, the owner of 'The Bend', and I am also the chef of this small shop. First off, I wasn't born into money. My father ran a small noodle restaurant for 50 years, and only retired a few years ago."

The mint potted plant he had just seen at the door suddenly appeared in his mind, and the small potted plant jumped dramatically in front of him, gently shaking its leaves, as if greeting and foretelling that a performance was about to begin.

Xiaoshu blinked, thought for a while, and asked, "Xinyi, something tells me that you are a person of stories. Your eyes radiate wisdom that is possible only in people who have been through much in life."

Lu Xinyi looked at Xiaoshu, smiled slightly. Her eyes drifted to a place far away, and she began to tell her story.

"I was once very fortunate. My family was typical, nothing out of the ordinary. My parents ran a small noodle restaurant that kept them busy all through the day and late into the night. Although we weren't rich, we weren't poor either. We could afford what we needed.

「你們好，是小樹跟知翔嗎？剛備好料，趁著空檔跟你們聊聊。我就是『轉角』的老闆盧心怡，也是這間小店的主廚。我先解釋：我不是富二代，我父親開了家小麵館，賣麵五十年，前幾年才退休。」

　　小樹腦海中突然浮現剛剛門口看到的薄荷盆栽，小盆栽在眼前戲劇性地跳了跳、輕輕搖了搖身上的薄荷葉子，好像打招呼、預告著準備要登場表演一樣。

　　小樹眨了眨眼睛、想了一會兒，問：「心怡姊，我覺得你應該是一個很有故事的人。你的眼睛散發出一種經歷過很多事，對人生看得很透澈的人，才會有的智慧光芒。」

　　盧心怡看向小樹，微微地一笑，眼神飄向遠處，輕聲地開始說故事：

　　「曾經，我是一個幸福的小女人。我的家庭很平常，爸爸媽媽開個小麵館，每天從一大早備料、煮麵、賣麵到善後清潔，忙到深夜。生活雖不算富裕，但物質上倒也不曾缺乏。

"After graduating, I got a job and married a co-worker. My husband loved me very much. We worked hard to hold the family together. Life was very simple, happy, and ordinary. We were also ready to start a family, perhaps one or two children, but unfortunately I didn't conceive.

"After three years of waiting and anticipation, my husband and I were very happy to welcome the arrival of a new life.

"But, in the second month of pregnancy, the fetus was found to have abnormal chromosomes and it had stopped growing. The child we had been wanting for three long years was gone in no time. I was completely devastated. The pain and discomfort in my body was nothing compared to the pain in my heart. The joy of pregnancy, before it even had the time to totally sinked in, was replaced by the bad news in a heartbeat. It was too cruel.

"My mother-in-law and my parents tried to comfort me at first, but what could I say or do that would be meaningful in response? After a while, when they met me, they watched me wordlessly, and even began to avoid me," she said. A trace of sadness flashed in Xinyi's eyes, and talking about the past brought her pain again.

「我畢業後找了份工作，就跟公司認識交往的同事結婚了。先生也很疼我，我們一起努力經營家庭，生活很簡單，幸福又平凡，也有準備要生養一兩個活潑可愛的孩子，可惜一直沒有懷孕的跡象⋯⋯

　　「等了三年，也盼了三年，終於像乾旱的大地等來了甘霖，我和先生都非常歡喜迎接新生命的到來。

　　「沒想到懷孕二個月，產檢時發現胎兒染色體異常，停止生長了。滿懷希望、盼了三年的孩子竟然就這麼沒了！當時真的是完全無法接受。身體的疼痛與不舒服，完全不能跟心裡的苦痛相比。得知懷孕的喜訊還沒消化完，就措手不及被噩耗狠狠打擊！

　　「苦盼著孫子的老人家，我的婆婆、我的父親母親剛開始都勸我安慰我，我只能苦笑，無法回應。日子一久，他們一遇到我就是無言哀戚地看著，甚至開始躲著我。」心怡眼神中閃過一絲悲哀，講起往事畢竟讓她再度陷入傷痛。

"I kept thinking that it must be my fault–something I did wrong or some signs I didn't notice and should havethat caused my child to stop growing. But exactly what went wrong? I couldn't figure it out, and I couldn't find the answer no matter how hard I looked for it. I became withdrawn, like a ghost without a voice, floating silently around the world, trying not to be noticed.

"Gradually, my husband came home late every day using every excuse imaginable, and some days he did even bother to come home at all. Maybe it's because he was afraid to talk to me–always crying–about the loss. That was our first child, and he must have been very sad and very disappointed, and he didn't know how to express himself.

"We were once warm and respectful to each other, but our relationship turned icy cold. We were once able to talk to each other about anything and everything, but we stopped talking to each other, like strangers. Eventually, for our common good, we ended our marriage."

Xiaoshu sensed Xinyi's heartache. He said softly, "Xinyi, that is life's impermanence, an accident, and a test, but that is definitely not anyone's fault"

「我覺得一定是因為我有什麼地方做得不對，沒注意到，孩子才停止長大。到底哪裡做錯了？我怎麼想都想不明白，怎麼找都找不到答案。我就像一個沒有聲音的鬼魂，默默地在人間飄來飄去，盡量不引起任何人的注意。

　　「漸漸地，先生每天用各種理由晚歸，甚至乾脆不回家。可能是因為害怕跟常常淚流滿面的我說話。這是我們的第一個孩子，他一定很難過也很失望，不知道該怎麼開口。

　　「我們夫妻倆從相敬如賓變成相敬如冰。從每天無話不談，變成不再對話的陌生人。最後為了彼此都能好好活下去，終究走上離婚這條路！」

　　小樹感應到心怡此時深陷回憶中內心的恐慌與苦悶，輕聲安慰：「心怡姊，這是無常、是意外、是考驗，但絕對不是任何人的錯。」

Lu Xinyi sighed, "I know it now, but I really didn't then, and I couldn't let go of it at first."

Xinyi pointed out that back then she was not herself, not fully anyway. One day crossing a street, absent-minded, she was hit by a car and was sent to the hospital with a foot injury.

"Incidents hitting me one after another almost shattered my heart beyond repair.

"On a bleak and cold night, I half limped and half dragged myself, like a zombie, slowly to the top floor of the hospital.In a daze, with difficulty breathing, I seriously considered whether I would jump off and end it all. But then I was worried that my aging parents would be saddened by the loss of me, and I was also afraid that my ex-husband would feel guilty about the loss of our child and about divorcing me and hence causing me to end my own life."

When Xinyi was anguished in her internal debate on whether to take a leap to her death, the head nurse, who had hurriedly followed Xinyin up the top floor, rushed up and put her arms tightly around Xinyi.

The head nurse said cheerfully, "Ancient poets were really wise when they wrote something like, 'If you want to see far, go up one flight of stairs'. Of all corners of the hospital, the

盧心怡嘆了口氣：「我現在知道了，但當初真的沒辦法放下。」

整天失魂落魄的心怡，在過馬路時，因為恍神竟出了車禍，被撞傷腳送進醫院。

「接二連三的事故打擊，幾乎讓我的心碎成一片片、再也無法拼湊完整。

「在一個淒淒冷冷的深夜，我拖著一瘸一瘸的傷腳，就像殭屍般，慢慢地走到醫院頂樓，發著呆、困難地呼吸、認真地考慮是不是要往下跳。卻又擔心年邁的父母因為失去我而傷心，也怕前夫內疚，覺得是因為離婚跟消失的孩子造成我想不開。」

心怡正在猶豫苦惱時，匆匆跟了上來的值班護理長趁心怡不注意，猛然抱住她。

護理長語氣開朗地說：「古人真的很有智慧，欲窮千里目、更上一層樓；行至水窮處、坐看雲起時。醫院

top floor commands the best view. I bet you're up here for the scenery."

Looking around from the top floor of the hospital, Xinyi could indeed see far and wide. By day, one can get a panoramic view of distant mountains, and by night you can see the lights from tens of thousands of homes. It's just beautiful.

At this time, the head nurse was enlightened: "Look at those little bits of light, each of those houses has a story all of its own."

Xinyi remembered the head nurse's soft laughter and words:

"Actually, everyone is a dot, and dots are connected to each other to form a line. So each dot is linked, directly or indirectly, to an infinite number of lines, which in turn form countless plains. Think about it, you can influence a lot of people!" She took Xinyi's hands as she continued.

"It is getting colder. I have some homemade hot ginger tea; it's delicious, and it is just right for this kind of weather. I have a little gift for you, too. So let's go."

Xinyi thought to herself: "She is so nice to me, and she shows up by my side when I need help the most." "The head nurse took me by the hand and slowly walked away from the

頂樓的風景最漂亮，你也是上來欣賞風景的吧！」

從醫院頂樓往四周看，視野遼闊，白天可以看得很遠，甚至可以欣賞到綿延的遠山，深夜裡也可以望向萬家燈火，和天上的星相互輝映，很美。

護理長此時又神來一筆：「看那一點一點燈光，每一家每一戶都有故事呢。」

心怡回憶著護理長的輕聲笑語：

「其實，每個人都是一個點，點跟點之間連成線，每個點都可以放射出無窮無盡的線，線再形成無數的面。想想看，你這個點可以影響很多人呢！」她牽起了心怡的手：

「天氣越來越冷了，我那邊有自製的熱薑茶，很好喝呢，這種天氣最適合了！還有一份小禮物要送你喔，我們一起走！」

怎麼會有這麼貼心的護理人員，而且在心怡最需要的時候出現在她身旁。「護理長牽著我的手，扶著我慢

edge of the building, and before I knew it, I was followingher downstairs."

Once downstairs, the head nurse gave Xinyi a small potted mint that was giving a faint, cool, and sweet scent that was very comforting. Then she took out the thermos flask, poured out a cup of steaming hot ginger tea, and said to Xinyi,

"Here is ginger tea. I made it myself. If you're under stress or got up on the wrong side of the bed, I recommend that you sniff the mint to refresh yourself or make mint tea."

Xinyi did as suggested and silently drank the cup of ginger tea.

"It's strange, but a warm stream of heat began to flow in my body, first from the stomach to the limbs, and then to the whole body. Finally, I was able to breathe normally!"

Xiaoshu and Zhixiang breathed a sigh of relief, and Zhixiang couldn't help but say, "That was a close one. Acting on the spur of the moment can cause lots of sorrow and regrets."

Xiaoshu had a flash of inspiration. He pursed his lips, smiled, and said,"I think I know the origin of the sweet potato ginger soup and lemon mint bubble drink." "Little Mint Potted Plant, I've heard your story. It turns out that you are a gift from the head nurse."

慢走，不知不覺就跟著她走下樓。」

下樓後，護理長送給心怡一個小盆栽，裡面種著清涼的薄荷，淡淡的清涼香甜味道，聞著十分舒服。接著又拿出隨身帶著的保溫瓶，倒出一杯冒著煙、熱騰騰的薑茶，一邊說：

「來！喝杯薑茶，我自己煮的。壓力來、心情不好的時候，建議聞聞薄荷，不但提神醒腦，還可以泡茶！」

心怡照著她的話，默默喝下了那杯薑茶，「奇特的，一股暖洋洋的熱流在我身體開始流動，從胃順著血液流到四肢，最後遊走全身，終於，我可以正常呼吸了！」

聽到這裡，小樹和知翔都大大地鬆了口氣，知翔忍不住說：「好險，很多遺憾都是因為一時衝動想不開造成的！」

小樹靈光一閃：「我想，我知道地瓜薑湯跟檸檬薄荷氣泡飲的出處了！」他偷偷地抿嘴笑：「小薄荷盆栽，我可聽到你的故事了！原來你就是護理長送的禮物。」

Lu Xinyi smiled softly and said slowly, "There is more to the story."

"When my father found out, he admonished me and told me the difference between disability and hindrance, both physical and mental. The formal means disability beyond repair and the latter disability that can be overcome. He said, 'You are very young, and you have a full life ahead of you. You silly girl, there are no hurdles in the world that cannot be overcome, only people who can't figure it out and can't let go.'"

Then, Xinyi's father told her a story.

He once met a customer who came to the restaurant to eat noodles but couldn't pay. "The young man was very pitiful. His boss owed him several months worth of wages; the factory was closed, and the proprietor had run away. The young man still had an old mother at home, and there was really no way for him to pay for the noodles. He asked if he could put the meal on the slate and he would pay it back when he found a job."

Without saying a word, Mr. Lu packed a few more orders of noodles, braised eggs, and side dishes for the young man, and asked him to take them back to eat with his mother. He also said to the young man, "Before you find a job, you come here to eat noodles when you are hungry, and you can pay

盧心怡溫柔地笑了笑，緩緩說：「故事還沒結束……」

　　「我父親知道後，又急又氣地念了我一頓。他說：你知道殘廢跟殘障有什麼不同？廢是報廢，但障是可以超越克服的困難！這麼年輕，未來有無限可能！傻孩子，世上沒有過不去的坎，只有想不通、放不下的人！」

　　接著，心怡的父親跟女兒講了個故事。

　　他曾經遇到一個到店裡來吃麵，卻付不出錢的顧客。「那個年輕人很可憐，老闆欠他幾個月的工資沒給，工廠關門了、老闆也跑路了。年輕人家裡還有老母親，實在沒辦法了，拜託盧老闆可不可以先賒帳給他，『等我找到工作一定會來還。』」

　　盧老闆二話不說直接再打包了幾包麵給他，還加上滷蛋、小菜，要他帶回去跟媽媽一起吃，還說，「這陣子找不到工作前，肚子餓就來店裡吃麵，將來有錢再

me back when you have money in the future." Other guests at the store all said that Mr. Lu was stupid, giving meals away without collecting money. But Xinyi's father could see that the young man was very honest and kind-hearted, and he would definitely work hard. He would not have eaten a meal without paying for it if it weren't absolutely necessary. Mr. Lu said to the young man, "You may come across a few bad people here and there, but the vast majority of the people in this world are good people. Don't lose your trust in people. Hope brings you strength and more hope. I encourage you to work hard."

Sure enough, Mr. Lu was right about that young man, who later became a very successful flower farmer, growing a lot of organic vegetables and fruits. He also had a greenhouse where he grew flowers and plants, and he had a beautiful garden.

Lu Xinyi said, "My dad suggested that I go to this young man, a Mr. Xie, because he and I both agreed that there is a lot of wisdom and energy in plants. I did go to Mr. Xie to work, where I learned a lot about planting and flower and plant cooking. Later, I opened 'The Bend', which had been my dream. I have dreamed about converting plants into something that can help people to cure the ills of their bodies and minds and to relaunch their lives after setbacks."

還。」其他客人都説盧爸爸真傻，哪有人不收錢還賠本送！但心怡的爸爸看得出年輕人很老實很善良，一定會認真工作，只是一時急缺，不是故意吃霸王餐。接著又鼓勵他：「這世界有少數不好的人，但大多數的都是好人，千萬不要失去你對人的信任。希望帶給你力量與希望，鼓勵你重新打拚、加油！」

　　果然，盧爸爸沒有看錯人，那位年輕人後來當了花農，種了很多有機蔬菜跟水果，做得很成功。他還種了一些溫室的花花草草，擁有一個非常美麗的花園。

　　「我爸建議我去找這個叫小謝的年輕人，因為他跟我都認同植物裡有很多學問跟能量，我後來真的去謝先生那裡工作跟學習，學會很多花草料理與栽種。後來，就開了『轉角』完成我的心願。將植物變成用來療癒身心的美食，也希望有機會讓人重新充電再出發！」

That's the end of Xinyi's story. "Okay, I need to go back to the kitchen to work, but you can stay and order whatever you like. Xiaoshu's cousin has already prepaid everything. And we offer discounts for frequent patrons."

Xiaoshu stopped Xinyi, "Please stay just a little longer. I want to ask one last question while we take a few more pictures. What about the name of the store 'The Bend'?"

Now Xiaoshu had all the information to complete the group report on "People and Things", except an ending.

Zhixiang clicked away and caught Lu Xinyi's bright smile.

"I am grateful for the trials and difficulties in my life, and I am even more grateful to those benefactors who have helped me learn to change my position and perspective and become a better person. I hope that at The Bend everyone can find the surprises after the river bend.

Challenges are plentiful and life's direction often bends. It's fair to say that bends abound in life, but how's the weather after the river bend? The weather can be anything you want to make it. Whatever comes your way, no matter how bad it may be, can bring you the most unexpected sorrow or joy–you, and you alone, decide which it will be.

心怡姊的故事講完了，「好，我得進去廚房準備飲料跟餐點了，你們再坐一下，隨意點你們喜歡的。小樹的大表哥已經先預付錢了，老客戶有折扣價喔。」

　　小樹喊住心怡：「請再等一下，在拍照的同時我想問最後一個問題，『轉角』這個店名……」

　　小樹把握時間追問，這篇「這些人那些事」小組故事報告資料已經很完整了，就差一個結尾！

　　喀擦一聲，知翔迅速按下快門，捕捉到盧心怡真誠燦爛的笑容。

　　「我感謝生命裡曾經出現過的考驗與困難，更謝謝那些幫助過我的貴人，讓我學會轉換立場與角度，成為一個更好的人。希望在轉角，大家都可以找到柳暗花明的另一片風景……」

　　人生何處不轉角？轉角的風景端看你當時的心情，晴雨都很美好，都可能是想不到的人生畫面。

The Magic of A Positive Attitude

The most terrible thing in life is not failures
or a lack of money.
It is losing heart and direction.
When you are confused, a benefactor may offer a good word
or a good thought.
Changing an angle or perspective can transform life.

正能量的磁場效應

人生最可怕的事，不是沒錢也不是失敗

而是對人生沒有了希望和失去方向

迷茫時，一位貴人一句好話一個好念

轉個角度換個高度，就能為生命帶來轉變的契機

第七章
CHAPTER 7

誰是好朋友？

Are you my buddy?

"Zhixiang, have you finished your homework for the winter break? I am still one report short." Xiaoshu asked as he swept fallen leaves into piles in a corner of the campus.

"Oh, aren't there still a few days left? Why are you in such a hurry?" Zhixiang replied while picking up garbage. "Xiaoshu, where are you going to go after the clean up?"

"I want to wander around for inspiration, but I haven't decided where to go yet," Xiaoshu said.

For the remaining report, Xiaoshu planned to write about drug prevention and control. A few days ago, he surfed the net for a bunch of information, such as news reports, flash cards, and videos, which at the time was nothing but disorganized raw data waiting to be gone over and organized. He had no idea on how to proceed yet. Suddenly he stopped what he was doing and stared at the floor.

"What's wrong? Is there money or gold on the ground?" Zhixiang moved closer for a better look.

"Look at the packaging of this jelly powder and coffee pod. Are they a little weird? They look a bit like something that I saw on the Internet," Xiaoshu frowned.

"I don't think I've ever heard of these brands. The powder in the bag also looks weird. There is also burned aluminum foil

「知翔，你寒假作業寫完了嗎？我還差一篇心得沒寫。」小樹一邊打掃校園角落的落葉，一邊問。

「哎呀，不是還有好幾天嗎，幹麼這麼著急？」知翔輕輕鬆鬆回答，手上撿垃圾的動作也沒停下來，「今天是半天的返校日，小樹，打掃完你準備去哪？」

「我想四處逛逛找靈感，還沒決定去哪……」

小樹的寒假作業打算寫跟毒品防治有關的心得。前幾天上網查了新聞報導、宣導圖卡懶人包、相關影片等一堆資料，現在還很雜亂，沒理出個頭緒，不知道要怎麼下筆。此時，小樹突然停下了手上的工作，看著地上發楞。

「怎麼了？地上是有錢還是有金幣啊？」知翔忍不住好奇，探過頭來。

「你看看地上這果凍粉跟咖啡包的包裝是不是有點怪怪的？跟我在網路上看到的資料有點像……」小樹皺起眉頭。

「這些牌子好像沒聽過？包裝袋裡的粉末看起來也

and a lighter next to it." Zhixiang bent down and looked at it for a moment. Shaking his head, he couldn't understand.

Xiaoshu picked up the package and aluminum foil from the spot that still had some loose powder lying around and studied it carefully. When he touched these strange things, his heart suddenly felt inexplicably heavy and beat faster. He sensed an attack by a vague human figure and a wave of negative emotions, making him feel just a little off the whole body over.

At first, he felt a little dizzy, experienced brain fog, and sensed his soul exiting his body. Then his stomach began to churn quite uncomfortably and his vision gradually became blurred. The images in front of him were crooked, his muscles were tense, and his consciousness was gradually dimming. Xiaoshu was very sure that his blood pressure was spiking, and his heart was about to jump out. He felt that he was going to suffocate. Then he fell into melancholy and inexplicable pessimism. He pinched the bag of residual powder packaging and aluminum foil in front of him, wanting to throw it out and yet grasping it tightly. He was at once filled with love and hate and all sorts of complicated emotions.

"Xiaoshu, are you all right?" Zhixiang, a little worried, shook the pale, rickety Xiaoshu.

怪怪的。旁邊還有燃燒過的鋁箔紙、打火機！」知翔彎下腰端詳了一下，搖搖頭，不懂。

小樹撿起地上還留有粉末的包裝袋與鋁箔紙仔細研究，當碰觸到這些陌生的東西時，突然心情莫名沉重起來，心跳加速，他感應到一個模糊的身影，伴隨著一股負面情緒襲來，整個人不太對勁。

剛開始有點暈眩，腦子茫茫然有種靈魂出竅感，之後腸胃開始扭曲起來很不舒服，漸漸視覺也模糊了，眼前影像歪七扭八地、渾身肌肉緊繃，意識漸漸模糊，小樹很清楚地意識到血壓上升，心臟蹦到快跳出來了，甚至有窒息感。最後，整個人陷入憂鬱和莫名的悲觀當中。他捏緊眼前那包殘留粉末包裝袋與鋁箔紙，想甩掉卻又抓緊緊，心底充滿又愛又恨、好複雜又好無奈的情緒！

「小樹，你還好吧？」知翔扶住臉色蒼白、搖搖晃晃的小樹，有些擔心。

It turned out that Xiaoshu was at a rapid speed sensing the journey of a drug user. When Xiaoshu returned to normal, he hurriedly put away the wrapping paper and aluminum foil, and said seriously, "No, we must tell the teacher. I sense that drugs are invading our campus. it's really despicable."

Zhixiang nodded and said, "I noticed a while back that strangers often lingered near our school. They got our classmates to a corner of campus doing something secret."

Xiaoshu looked around for something. "There are no surveillance cameras here, so it is a blind spot on campus," Xiaoshu said, "The smell of burned plastic or the sight of small zipper bags with powder residue or burned aluminum foil and lighters anywhere on campus may indicate that drugs have reached the campus. After reporting to the teacher on duty, let's go and take a closer look, shall we?"

Zhixiang hesitated a little at first, but after taking a good look at Xiaoshu, he said, "Okay, I am free, so let's do it."

After carefully rummaging and collecting evidence, Xiaoshu and Zhixiang went to the teacher on duty and reported what they had found. The teacher praised them for being vigilant and said that she would alert the principal, the school council, and the police.

其實，小樹當時正以飛快的速度感應了一回毒品使用者的歷程。當被知翔喚醒恢復正常後，小樹趕忙把包裝紙與鋁箔紙收起來，神情嚴肅地說：「不行，一定要報告老師，應該是有毒品入侵校園，真是太可惡了！」

知翔點點頭，回憶：「我注意到前陣子有陌生人經常在學校附近探頭探腦，還約同學鬼鬼祟祟地躲在角落，不知在幹麼？」

小樹警覺看向四周：「這裡沒有監視器，算是校園死角。」他分享看過的資料跟知翔討論：「教室、廁所及校園死角如果有燃燒塑膠的異味、殘留不明粉末的小夾鏈袋，或垃圾桶內有燃燒過的鋁箔紙、打火機，都有可能是毒品問題。我們不能讓毒品進入校園毒害大家！待會跟值班老師報告後，我們再去仔細找看看好嗎？」

知翔剛開始有點遲疑，深深地看了一眼小樹後，鼓起勇氣：「好，反正我等下也沒事，一起行動。」

經過仔仔細細地翻找與蒐集證據，小樹和知翔結伴去跟值班老師報告，留下文字紀錄，「老師稱讚我們很有警覺心，她會把今天我們找到的東西報告校長和校務會議，也會報警處裡。」

A sense of achievement made Xiaoshu and Zhixiang feel pretty good.

"The teacher also said that treatment after the fact is far less effective than prevention beforehand. We should care more about our classmates and friends and give them more positive energy. This may prevent them from being tempted to go down the road of no return," Xiaoshu said very seriously.

"By the way, why did Wenquan ask for leave on the day of returning to school? Is he sick?" Wenquan and Xiaoshu have been good friends since kindergarten, but at this time, the thought of Wenquan unsettled Xiaoshu no end.

"Wenquan said that he asked for leave because he didn't sleep well and his head hurt," Zhixiang said, "I think Wenquan has been a little weird lately, often in a daze with an expression that I don't know how to describe. He seemed to be hurting. Sometimes I called him by name and said hello to him, but he didn't respond as if he didn't hear it."

"My impression of Wenquan is that he is not much of a talker, but he is kind at heart. Once a classmate almost fainted because he had not eaten breakfast and his blood sugar was too low. Wenquan immediately gave his own bread to him. I think he's a good person. Something must have happened for him

小樹和知翔覺得很有成就感。

「老師還講，事後的治療遠不如事前的預防來得更重要、更有成效。我們應該多關心身邊的同學跟朋友，多給他們正能量，避免他們受到誘惑走上不歸路。」小樹非常認真地說。

「對了，文泉怎麼返校日還請假？他生病了嗎？」文泉是小樹自幼稚園就同學的好朋友，但這會兒提到文泉的名字，小樹心頭突然浮現亂糟糟的情緒，憂傷又無奈的感覺，整個人被拉扯著很難受，無力的雙腳正瑟瑟發抖，好像站在洶湧而來的浪濤前面，一不小心就會被強大的感傷與憤恨席捲而去。

「班長說，文泉今天一大早就跟他說因為沒睡好、頭很痛，所以請假！」知翔眉頭開始皺起來：「我覺得文泉最近怪怪的，常常發呆，他的表情我不太會形容，好像很難過的樣子。對了，我有時叫他名字、跟他打招呼，他都不理，也不知道是真的沒聽見還是怎樣？」

「我對文泉的印象是，他雖然話不多，可是心地善良。上次班長因為沒吃早餐，血糖過低差點昏倒，他馬上拿自己的麵包給班長吃。我覺得他人不錯，最近會這

to act weird lately," Xiaoshu said to Zhixiang, "Do you know where Wenquan lives? Let's pay him a visit."

Zhixiang nodded and said, "Yes. He is a single-parent kid raised by his grandma. He has no siblings. His father works in a factory and usually lives in the factory dormitory. I know where his house is."

The two of them hurried to Wenquan's home.

Wenquan answered the door. He looked listless and seemed unable to open his eyes. He was very surprised by the surprise visit. To keep the bright sun from his face, he just wanted to hide behind the door.

"Wenquan, let's take a walk to the river embankment. We can chat and exercise a little. They are good for our health," Xiaoshu said.

"I have some sandwiches and sports drinks. I guarantee you won't get bored," Zhixiang also urged him on.

The two of them half dragged a reluctant Wenquan out the door. Xiaoshu said, "I really like to find time to bask in the sun, enjoy the breeze, and add a little vitamin D from nature."

"It's like a whim, a little outing that you can just go to, it's very interesting!" Xiaoshu said.

樣，應該是發生了什麼事。」小樹停下腳步，跟知翔建議：「你知道文泉家住哪嗎？一起去看一下。」

知翔馬上點頭，補充他所知道的文泉家的狀況：「他好像是隔代的單親家庭，被奶奶帶大的，家裡也沒其他兄弟姊妹，爸爸在工廠上班、平常住在工廠宿舍。我知道他家在哪。」

兩人腳步匆匆，探望文泉去。

敲開文泉家的大門，一副沒精打采、睜不開貓熊眼的文泉「啊！」了一聲，很吃驚，沒想到同學來訪，刺眼的陽光讓他一時之間只想躲在門後頭。

「文泉，我們一起去河堤散散步、聊聊天，稍微運動一下，對身體比較好！」小樹說道。

「我準備了三明治和運動飲料，保證不會無聊！」知翔也在一旁鼓吹。

兩人硬拉著有些不情願的文泉出門，小樹說道：「我超喜歡找空檔曬曬太陽、吹吹風，補充一點來自大自然的維他命D。」

「這就好像是心血來潮、說走就走的小郊遊，很有意思吧！」小樹說。

"Next time, we can play ball or go biking." Zhixiang said.

"Take time to participate in activities, meet different people, and learn about a lot of things, and they will make life more exciting." Xiaoshu continued.

The two of them kept saying things to interest Wenquan for fear that he would turn around and go home.

"BTW, guess what we found this morning while sweeping the campus. It was like Conan's Sherlock Holmes story. Too bad you weren't there," Zhixiang deliberately piqued his curiosity.

Wenquan looked lost, so Zhixiang told the story in great detail of what had happened when he swept the school in the morning. Xiaoshu noticed that Wenquan's expression changed whenever Zhixiang mentioned drugs and drug use, and he looked very uncomfortable and defensive, crossing his arms in front of his chest.

When Zhixiang came to a stop, Xiaoshu said slowly, "Many people have come into contact with drugs. At first they are just curious or influenced by friends, and they don't have a clue how serious the consequences are."

Wenquan looked thoughtful as he lowered his arms and stared into the distance. He sighed and said, "I know everything

「下次我們也可以約去打球或騎車喔。」知翔説。

「有空多出來參加活動，可以看到不一樣的人，學到很多事，會讓生活更精采。」小樹接著説道。

只見兩人你一言我一語的，生怕文泉不接受，就輪番端出許多好玩有趣的誘因讓他出門。

「對了！你還不知道，上午我們在打掃校園時發現了什麼，簡直像名偵探柯南玩冒險遊戲呢。可惜你沒來，錯過了精采的部分！」知翔故意賣關子。

看著一臉茫然的文泉，知翔就把上午返校打掃時的經過鉅細靡遺地講一遍。小樹注意到當知翔提到毒品、吸毒這些關鍵字眼時，文泉表情起了變化，神情很不自在，兩手交叉在胸前，十分防備的樣子。

等知翔說到一個段落，小樹接著緩緩説道：「很多人接觸毒品，一開始都只是好奇或被朋友影響，不了解後遺症有多嚴重。」

這時文泉露出若有所思的表情，兩手逐漸垂下，他看著遠方深嘆一口氣：「我知道，我都知道，我叔叔就

about drugs. My uncle is a heavy drug addict, and he is still in prison. Our family has been thoroughly shattered by drugs!"

Zhixiang was very surprised. Xiaoshu nodded, and gingerly said, "If you talk to your friends about your troubles and ask them to help, maybe the troubles will be less suffocating."

"That's right! Three people have more ideas and more strength than one."

Wenquan smiled wryly and said, "Our family was not rich, but we were able to put food on the table and clothes on our backs. Our lives were ordinary but happy. Grandpa was in poor health and passed away very early. Grandma is very warm, always wearing kind smiles. My dad is the first child. My grandparents always wanted him to be a good role model, so they set strict rules in raising him, and he always did what was expected of him and never did anything that would run against Grandpa and Grandma's will."

In one breath, Wenquan told them all these things–secrets that he had never before shared with anyone. "But my uncle is different. He often got sick as a child, so my grandparents took special care of him. They didn't ask him to help with things, and they didn't require him to maintain any particular GPA at school. After my grandfather passed away, my grandmother

是一個重度吸毒成癮的人，現在還在監獄裡，我們家就是被毒品害到變得這樣破碎！」

知翔非常驚訝，小樹點點頭，小心翼翼地試探說道：「有時候把煩惱說出來，讓朋友幫忙分擔，也許就不會那麼煩了！」

「對呀！三個人比一個人點子多、力量大。」

文泉苦笑一下說：「我們家算不上是有錢人，但還算是衣食無缺，日子原本過得平凡幸福。爺爺身體不好，很早就過世了。奶奶是個非常溫暖的人，笑起來非常親切。我爸是老大，爺爺奶奶總要他當個好榜樣，所以管教非常嚴格；他從小就很聽話，從來不會違背爺爺奶奶的要求。」

文泉一口氣說出他從沒跟人說過的這些事：「我叔叔就不一樣了，因為小時候身體很不好，常生病，所以爺爺奶奶對他特別照顧，也沒要求他幫忙做事，也不會管他成績一定要怎樣。爺爺過世後，奶奶因為擔心叔叔

was more tolerant of my uncle because she was worried about his health. After my father graduated from high school, she asked my father to work part-time in a factory to help support the family."

"Your dad is really sensible and responsible," Xiaoshu said in much admiration. However, Zhixiang had an opinion about the double standard of Wenquan's grandma in bringing up her two sons, so he said, "I think it is unfair to treat two children so differently."

"Uncle is not in good health, so everyone always tolerated his irresponsible behavior and put up with his thoughtless actions. No matter what trouble he had caused, Grandma would always help him find an excuse and ask everyone to forgive him. Once my uncle stole a pencil case from a classmate and the teacher informed Grandma; Grandmother went to the school to apologize to the teacher and the classmate on his behalf. But such indulgence only emboldened my uncle. He stole class petty cash and classmates' watches, and he beat people up. Grandmother went to school to kneel down in front of the teacher to apologize, to beg the principal to give my uncle another chance. Even my father couldn't look past it and wanted to discipline him, but my grandmother cried to stop

的健康，所以對叔叔更加寬容，還要求我爸中學畢業就到工廠半工半讀，幫忙賺錢養家。」

「你爸真懂事，很有責任感。」小樹很佩服。但知翔則對文泉奶奶對兩個兒子的差別教育有意見：「我覺得對兩個孩子的管教態度差這麼多，不公平。」

「叔叔因為身體不好，大家總是讓他三分，不管他做了什麼，奶奶總是會幫他找理由，要大家原諒他。甚至有一次，叔叔在學校偷拿了同學的鉛筆盒，被老師告到家裡來，奶奶也會出面去學校，幫他跟老師和同學道歉。但叔叔越來越大膽，偷班費、偷同學的手錶、打人，奶奶還去學校跟老師下跪道歉，求主任給叔叔機會，連我爸看不過去要管教，都被奶奶哭著阻止。」文泉語氣

him," Wenquan said resignedly.

"Gee. If a child isn't disciplined for bad behavior, he is surely to become a little terror," Xiaoshu said.

"He could never know that his behavior was bad. Grandma was his backer," Zhixiang added.

"Later, my parents got married and I came along, and our new family moved to Southern Taiwan, and we rarely came back to visit Grandma. But Dad would send money back to Grandma on time every month," Wenquan said, "Grandma couldn't rein in my uncle, and she didn't have the heart to do so. Therefore, my uncle was totally free to do as he pleased."

"I hope that your uncle later became more sensible and learned to take responsibility for himself," Xiaoshu said, a little anxiously.

"I'm afraid that an undisciplined brat making small troubles will grow into a thud making big troubles," Zhixiang shook his head violently.

Wenquan said, "Grandma had hoped that my uncle would marry a good wife, and after having children, he would become mature and sensible, so she had enlisted the service of matchmakers and blind dates. Finally, he got a girlfriend, got married, and gave birth to a son, which was normally

十分無奈。

「唉！犯錯不教，恐怕會寵成小霸王了。」

「這樣他會知道自己錯了嗎？奶奶變成靠山了！」小樹、知翔你一言我一語。

「後來我爸媽結婚生下我，搬到南部住，就很少回來。但爸爸每個月都會按時寄錢回來給奶奶。」文泉輕聲嘆氣：「奶奶管不動也不忍心管，我爸又有自己的家庭要顧，叔叔就更自由了！」

「希望你叔叔長大後，能懂事一點，學會為自己負責。」小樹有點著急。

「只怕沒有人管教的小麻煩長大了，變成大麻煩就糟了！」知翔猛搖頭。

「奶奶希望叔叔找個好老婆，結婚生子後或許會變得成熟懂事，所以一直安排他相親。好不容易等到他交了女朋友，結了婚，也生了兒子，這時卻發生一件大

very good news for the family. But just then a big event happened," Wenquan frowned and said, "Uncle made a group of fair-weather friends, who often partied in bars all night. Surrounded by friends who smoked cigarettes laced with ketamine, my uncle took a puff of it–his first–which embarked him on the road of no return. Ketamine, amphetamine, and an assortment of drugs all found their way into his daily life. Then he became a drug dealer. He was all in, and he was up to his ears in drugs. And that is his story."

So drawn into the story that Zhixiang lamented for and became angry at Wenquan's uncle, "He could have a good life, but he chose to give up on himself."

"Your uncle has been loved and spoiled since he was a child, but doing drugs is serious and consequential. Why didn't anyone intervene?" Xiaoshu asked suspiciously.

"There were attempts to pull my uncle back from drugs, but he simply would not change his way. His wife quarreled with him about it all day long, and at times their quarrels turned so physically violent that pots and pans would fly across the kitchen and glasses would be smashed. Back then, because my parents divorced, I was sent back to live with my grandmother, my uncle, and his wife. Every day the shouting, screaming,

事……」文泉眉頭緊鎖，「叔叔結交了一群喜歡吃喝玩樂的朋友，常在酒吧聚會整晚狂歡。看著朋友一個個抽著含 K 他命的菸吞雲吐霧，一時好玩就從此踏上不歸路！拉 K、安非他命、吸毒、最後走上販毒，結果越陷越深，唉，這就是他的故事！」

原來如此，令人不禁感嘆！但知翔還是很氣憤：「真是很糟糕！明明生活可以往好的方向轉變，沒想到他卻這麼自暴自棄！」

「你叔叔從小被疼愛被寵到大，但是吸毒這麼嚴重的事怎麼都沒人出面管管？」小樹很疑惑地問道。

「誰說沒管，是管不動啊！嬸嬸整天跟他大吵，家裡鍋碗瓢盆飛來飛去，玻璃也砸碎。那幾年因為我爸媽離婚，我被送回來給奶奶照顧，每天都被各種大呼小叫、

fighting, and crying of my uncle and his wife, my aunt, scared me to death. My home was anything but homey. My aunt cried every time she saw me, and she kept shouting that she had married the wrong man, a mistake for which she was paying with the happiness of herself and her son," Wenquan's blank eyes looked into the distance and said helpless, "My uncle insisted that his friends would not harm him, and he kept asking for money to buy drugs at every turn, draining the cash in the family. He could sell, steal, or pawn anything of value at home just so he could buy more drugs. Grandma couldn't bear to see him suffering, so she secretly gave him money out of the living expenses—money that Dad sent to her every month."

"She continued to give him money? The way addicts spend money on drugs means that she was throwing money in a bottomless pit," Xiaoshu said.

"The more drug addicts use, the more addicted they become, and in the end, they become drug dealers," Zhixiang said.

Xiaoshu said to Wenquan, "Are your aunt and cousin okay?"

"My aunt ran away from home with her son after a big argument and a big fight with my uncle. We couldn't locate them to inform them of the news that my uncle had been put

嘶吼哭鬧的場面嚇得半死，家裡氣氛很差，嬸嬸每次看到我就哭得淚流不止，一直喊說她看錯人，誤了自己一輩子也害了我堂弟！」文泉兩眼無神看著遠處，十分無助，「我叔叔堅持朋友不會害他，動不動就伸手要錢買毒，家裡的現金、能賣的能偷的能拿的，全被他拿去換毒品了。奶奶因為不忍心，還把我爸爸寄來的生活費也偷偷拿了一些給叔叔用。」

「還拿錢給他？吸毒的人花錢如流水，永遠也填不滿無底洞！」

「毒品越用越重，到最後就是會去販毒，越陷越深啊。」知翔、小樹不約而同地說，話頭一轉，小樹表達關心地問道：

「那你嬸嬸和堂弟還好嗎？」

「嬸嬸在一次跟叔叔大吵大鬧、動手打架過後，帶著堂弟離家出走了。連叔叔後來坐牢也不知怎麼通知她們。一個單親媽媽要獨力照顧小孩本來就很不容易。我

in jail. It is not easy for a single mother to raise her children on her own. My dad and I were very worried, and we tried every way possible to find them to no avail. Later, I heard about them. It seems that they have changed their names and have a new life, and they just want to forget that horrible period of their lives with my uncle. I don't know if it's true or not."

"The child is innocent!"

"Drug addiction is really bad for your uncle and his family!" Xiaoshu and Zhixiang were very sad when they heard it.

"Not only that, but my grandmother used to take a bus all the way to visit her son in prison, and she cried all the time when she saw her son. When she came back, she stared blankly at the sky and muttered to herself, 'Am I wrong? I love him so much which hurt him instead. Did I handle it the wrong way?' Sometimes I hear my grandmother sobbing in the middle of the night, and I can't sleep all night." Wenquan's eyes were red, and tears were rolling in his eyes.

"Not only is my grandmother listless all the time, but she is getting weaker by the day. Her dementia has been getting worse and worse since last year. She often gets lost, not remembering where her home is, and her speech shows her confusion. She always gets confused about time and space, and at the end of

跟我爸都很擔心，曾經透過各種管道尋找她們，但是都沒有結果！後來輾轉打聽到，好像她們改了名字、有了新生活、不想提過去，也不知是真是假？」

「孩子很無辜！」

「吸毒真是害慘了你叔叔和他的家庭！」小樹、知翔聽了都好難過。

「不只這樣，奶奶之前自己大老遠搭車去監獄探望她兒子，看著叔叔就一直哭。回來她就呆呆地看著天空，喃喃地嘶啞自問：『我錯了嗎？我這麼愛他卻害了他，是我錯了嗎？』有時半夜聽到奶奶的啜泣聲，我整夜也都沒法睡著。」文泉眼眶發紅，淚水在眼裡打轉。

「奶奶不只時刻無精打采，整個人沒了生氣，身體也一天天變得衰弱。去年開始，她的失智狀況越來越嚴重！經常迷路、記不得自己家在哪，講話顛三倒四，一

last month, she fell at the door of our house and hit her head. She passed away two days later at the hospital," said a tearful Wenquan.

"It's a pity that her life ended this way," Zhixiang said.

"I'm sure your uncle must be upset, too," Xiaoshu said.

"Two weeks ago, my father visited my uncle in the prison and told him that Grandma had passed away and the final arrangement had been made. My uncle applied for a funeral leave. Upon coming home, he knelt down in front of Grandma's portrait and bitterly cried, crying his heart out. He said that Grandma had loved him and spoiled him rotten since he was little, had always tried to get him out of the bind or explained his bad behavior away, that he didn't know why he had behaved the way he had and why he had strayed, that now his family had left him and Grandma, his number one fan and backer, was gone, too, that he couldn't come home to care for Grandma when she was ill, that he regretted it all very much. He continued to say that he wanted to repent, but it was all too late," said Wenquan, his head lowered, "His regret came too late, but Dad urged my uncle to see drugs for what they really were and to renounce them. Dad told him that the right way forward and a new life are his for the asking. Dad said to him,

直把時間跟空間搞混，上個月底在房門口摔了一大跤、撞到頭後送去醫院，隔兩天就過世了！」文泉講到這裡，淚眼滿眶。

「奶奶好可憐喔。」知翔也難過起來。

「我相信你叔叔應該也很難過。」小樹生起同理心。

「前兩個星期我爸去探監跟他講奶奶死了，也安排好喪事，叔叔趕忙申請手續回來奔喪，他在奶奶的遺像前下跪痛哭，聲嘶力竭地泣訴，說奶奶從小就很疼他，什麼事都幫他想好退路，闖了禍都有奶奶倚靠解決，他不知道自己怎麼會變成這樣！現在家沒了，靠山也沒了，他很後悔，連奶奶生病時，都無法回來照顧奶奶，他很懺悔，但一切都來不及了！」文泉低下頭來：「這個悔恨來得太晚了！我爸勸叔叔回頭是岸，知錯能改。

'You've got a brother here. I will visit you and wait for your release," Wenquan said.

"A good family and a good life were ruined by drugs. Hindsight is always 20/20," Zhixiang said, shaking his head.

"I've read that drugs are horrifying. They are extremely habit-forming; it's exceedingly difficult to rid the addiction once it has been formed, and drugs will also cause great harm to their users, such as complications of the digestive and immune systems, damage to the nervous system and organs, diminished brain function, and even death," Xiaoshu said, "A person who has just started taking drugs is like a fly in a glass jar–seeing the bright and alluring world outside but totally unable to find a way out!"

Wenquan suddenly raised his head and said, "So as soon as I heard the words drugs and drug use, I went crazy," clenching his fists, he continued, "Grandma was really nice, and she would secretly stuff fruits, candies, and biscuits into my pockets at every chance, for fear that I would go hungry. She would tell me at every chance to put on more clothes so as not to catch a cold. I didn't expect her to pass away so soon after she fell, and I really regret that I didn't spend more time with

他對叔叔說：你還有哥哥，哥哥去探望你，等你出來的那一天。」

「千金難買早知道！好好一個家、一個人生，就因為毒品整個毀了！」知翔搖頭嘆息。

小樹分享透過各種資訊得來有關毒品對健康的傷害：「聽說毒品很可怕，除了成癮性極高，一旦接觸到就很難擺脫，而且還會對吸食者的身體造成極大傷害，像是消化系統、免疫系統的多種併發症都會發生，還會造成神經、器官受損、腦力鈍化、甚至還會殘害生命。」他還用了這樣的比喻：「剛開始吸食毒品的人，就像是一隻趴在玻璃上的蒼蠅，心情上可能暫時一片光明，但其實是找不到出路的！」

文泉這會兒突然抬起頭來，「所以我一聽到毒品、吸毒這些字眼，整個人就快抓狂了！」他握緊了拳頭，「我奶奶人真的很好，每次都會偷偷塞水果、糖果跟餅乾給我，生怕我餓著了。每次也會叮嚀我多穿點，不要著涼感冒。沒想到她跌倒後這麼快就走了，我真後悔以

her and comfort her. At least I should have told her that I love her very much."

Wenquan wiped his tears, regretting and wondering about many should haves and could haves. Again, hindsight is always 20/20.

Zhixiang tried to lighten the air, so he said, "No wonder there is a kind of hunger called grandma's hunger, so named because grandmas keep putting food in front of their grandkids. No wonder Wenquan has difficulties losing weight, thanks to his grandma's pampering."

Xiaoshu said, "My grandfather started living with us a while back. Because my parents are very busy and I have to go to school, we take him to a daycare center. When he is at home, he often repeatedly asks the same question, and he often confuses me with my dad. I will become very impatient with him when he asks too many questions, and I will raise my voice or give him an attitude. Listening to Wenquan's talk about his grandma, I need to seriously change and be kind and more patient with Grandpa."

Thinking of something, Zhixiang said, "Last month, someone gave out free chocolates near the school entrance. Did you get any?"

前沒有多陪陪她、安慰她。至少我應該要告訴奶奶，我很愛她。」

文泉擦著眼淚，又是一個後悔的人生──千金難買早知道！

知翔想轉換氣氛，「難怪人家說：有一種餓，叫阿媽覺得你很餓，所以一直要你多吃。文泉瘦不下來的原因，是因為阿媽照顧得太好了！」

小樹想起了自己的爺爺：「我爺爺前陣子開始住我家，爸媽很忙我也要上學，所以爺爺常常要被送去日照中心。他在家時，一個問題常常重複問好幾次，還經常把我和我爸弄錯。」小樹臉紅地解釋：「被問多了，我會很不耐煩，態度跟口氣都很差地大聲跟爺爺回話。聽文泉講奶奶的事，我認真反省應該要對爺爺好一點、更有耐心才對！」

知翔想起一件事：「上個月有人放學在校門口附近分送免費的巧克力，請大家吃看看，你們有拿到嗎？」

Xiaoshu said nervously, "Capsules, jelly, or coffee pods, fruit juice powder, gummies, popping candy, chocolate, noodles, plum chips, soft drinks, loquat paste, and so on. These and other similar items with unfamiliar pseudo-packaging may be drugs."

Wenquan also asked nervously, "Zhixiang didn't eat it, did you?"

"I put it in my pocket. Then I thought the packaging was a little weird, so I didn't want to eat it. In the end, I threw it away."

Xiaoshu said, "I heard from volunteer Team Leader Wu that there will be a seminar on 'Drugs and I don't see eye to eye' put on by a very experienced anti-drug advocacy group, and we will have an opportunity to see them after the school starts. Want to go with us?"

"Okay, Sounds interesting." Wenquan said loudly, "Count me in!"

In an instant, Xiaoshu, Wenquan, and Zhixiang saw eye to eye on drugs.

A true good friend can see his own strengths and weaknesses, and he can also see a better self.

小樹很緊張：「來源不明的膠囊、果凍或咖啡包、果汁粉、軟糖、跳跳糖、巧克力、科學麵、梅片、汽水、枇杷膏等等，這些類似的偽包裝都有可能是毒品。」

　　文泉也跟著緊張地問：「知翔沒吃吧？」

　　「我放進口袋，覺得包裝有點怪，不敢吃，後來就丟了！」

　　小樹突然想到：「我聽志工吳小隊長說有一個教育宣導團，好像叫『無毒有我，有我無毒』，他們經常舉辦許多反毒教育的宣導活動，開學後我們有機會一起去看好嗎？」

　　「好，我有興趣！」文泉也大聲說：「算我一個！」

　　小樹感受文泉與知翔的活力與決心，三個人的影子緊連在一起，在黃昏的地上拉得好長好長。

　　真正的好朋友，可以照見自己的優點與不足，更能夠照見更好的自己。

The Magic of A Positive Attitude

A true friend shows genuine concern.
Let your friends know that you care about their health and
future.
If you care about your friends, offer them more than criticism
or accusations.
Show them also your concerns for them and provide them
with specific assistance at the right moments.
Also make sure that you remain upstanding and protected.

正能量的磁場效應

作為真正的朋友，要表現出真誠的關心
讓朋友知道你關心他們的健康和未來
關心朋友不應該僅止於批評或指責
適時提出關心的問題，提供具體的幫助
同時也要確保你自己的心理健康

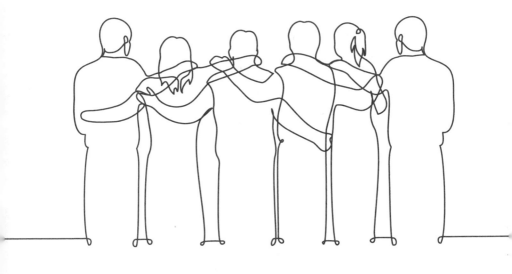

第八章
CHAPTER 8

老後的時光

In our later years

Xiaoshu had a nightmare on one Sunday night. Though it was vivid, he woke up remembering nothing about it at all. Looking around, he suddenly caught a glimpse of the family photo hanging on the wall and sensed that his grandfather in the photo looked haggard, as if he was sick. He hurried to get out of bed. Just then, the phone rang. His father answered the phone, but he immediately turned nervous. After hanging up, his father said that it was from his grandfather's doctor, saying that the grandpa might have chronic anxiety disorder and that he needed to be accompanied.

Xiaoshu's grandfather, 78, lives alone in his countryside home. He once ran a plumbing business. After he hung it up, he and Grandma took sightseeing tours abroad often for a while, but he has rarely left home for a year since Grandma passed. Xiaoshu's father repeatedly asked him to move to live with them, but he simply refused again and again. Now the doctor of Xiaoshu's grandfather had called, and things didn't look good. Xiaoshu's father made up his mind to bring Xiaoshu's grandfather back to his home. Xiaoshu's father put a big, empty suitcase in the trunk, and Xiaoshu joined his father as they drove off to the grandfather's house.

星期假日，小樹做了一個噩夢，夢境歷歷如生，但醒來卻完全不記得了。瞧瞧四周，小樹忽然瞥見牆上掛著的全家福合照，感應到照片裡爺爺神色憔悴，好像生病了。他趕緊起床。此時，電話鈴響，爸爸接完電話口氣很緊張，說是爺爺的醫生打來的，說爺爺可能得了慢性焦慮症，需要人陪伴。

　　小樹回憶起，七十八歲的爺爺一個人住鄉下，以前開水電工程行，退休後跟奶奶出國玩了一陣子，但自從奶奶去世後，這一年都不太想出門，無論爸爸怎麼請他過來一起住，爺爺就是不願意。這次小樹和爸爸拉了一個大大、騰空的行李箱，下決心一定要把爺爺接回來。

It was a long drive. They just grabbed something quick to eat along the way, and, six hours later, they reached Xiaoshu's grandfather's house. As soon as Xiaoshu opened the door, He saw Xiaoshu's grandfather half-lying on the sofa in the living room, his hands touching his chest and saying that he had chest tightness. He didn't sleep well last night, leaving him dizzy, void of appetite, and hardly any vitality. Xiaoshu's grandfather had always been tidy, but now his house was filthy with things. There was no rancid smell, but there were many empty boxes, cardboard boxes, and broken electrical appliances. Xiaoshu's father sat next to Xiaoshu's grandfather, opened a boxed meal and tried to feed him. He gingerly asked Xiaoshu's grandfather to move with him to his house up north. Surprisingly, Xiaoshu's grandfather agreed to try it, although only for a month at first. Xiaoshu could see that Xiaoshu's grandfather still liked the leisurely and quiet life in the countryside.

Xiaoshu's grandfather's surprising consent prompted Xiaoshu's father and Xiaoshu to rush to pack a few of Xiaoshu's grandfather's things and throw away his worn-out socks and towels, which they could buy easily enough when they got home. Xiaoshu saw a special toothbrush that had

開車出發，父子倆沿途買了便當充飢，花了六小時才到爺爺家。一開門，看到爺爺半躺在客廳沙發上，手摸著胸口說很悶，老人家昨天沒睡好，全身沒力，頭暈眼花，也沒食慾。爺爺算是愛乾淨的人，但如今家裡竟堆滿了東西，雖然沒有什麼腐臭味，但空盒子、紙箱與壞了的電器用品特別多，小樹的爸爸坐在爺爺身旁，打開便當，試著餵他吃，邊試圖說服爺爺搬來都市跟他們同住，爺爺答應先住一個月看看，因他還是喜歡鄉下悠緩安靜的生活。

　　難得爺爺答應了，小樹與爸爸連忙整理了一箱衣物，舊毛巾、牙刷之類就丟掉，等北上再買新的。就在這當下，小樹看到一支比較特別的牙刷，密密的細毛，

dense fine bristles and a discolored handle, which he promptly threw in the trash can as well. He asked Xiaoshu's grandfather what to do with those empty boxes, cartons, and recyclables. He scratched his head as he was at a loss as to what to do. Moments later he said, "I usually sort them out nicely and put them outside. Someone would collect them, and they'd give me a little pocket money."

In this way, Xiaoshu's grandfather left his house where he had lived alone and went to Xiaoshu's father 's house in the north.

But after just a few days, Xiaoshu noticed that Xiaoshu's grandfather was looking for things all day long. When he couldn't find them, he became anxious, his slightly trembling hands kept rummaging through all of his belongings, constantly wiping sweat, and pacing the house. Xiaoshu's father was very patient, though. He drove him to a nearby supermarket to buy what Xiaoshu's grandfather couldn't find at home. But it only took a few days for the cycle to repeat itself.

One day, Xiaoshu's grandfather said that he didn't like his toothbrush. He thought of the toothbrush with dense bristles that he had used in the past. Xiaoshu remembered seeing and throwing away that old toothbrush, but Xiaoshu looked for it

把柄都脫色了，於是也順手丟進垃圾桶。那麼那些空盒子、紙箱、回收品呢？爺爺說：「真糟糕，我的腦袋好像生鏽了一樣，突然不知道要怎麼整理啦？」他又想了想，說：「對了，我都整理好放外面有人會來收，他們會給我一點零用錢。」

就這樣，爺爺離開一個人住的老家，跟著兒孫北上，也添購了些日常用品。

但住沒幾天，小樹發現爺爺整天都在找東西，找不到人就焦慮起來，不停地用微微顫抖的手來回翻遍所有家當、不停地擦汗、不停地來回踱步。小樹的爸爸很有耐心，開車載老人家去附近超商再買他找不到的東西。但常常都是剛買回家，沒幾天又找不到了，就又去買，就這樣來來回回好多次。

有一天，爺爺說他現在的牙刷不好用，想起來以前那支密密刷毛的牙刷！小樹看過，知道爺爺形容的樣

in nearby stores to no avail. He could not find it online, either. Xiaoshu's grandfather said that he could buy that kind of toothbrush at a grocery store near his house. Oh, no. That's a very long trip just for some toothbrushes.

Xiaoshu planned the trip in his head. If he took the bus to the bus terminal and changed to a long-haul bus, it would take more than 5 hours to reach Xiaoshu's grandfather's house. The thought of spending so much time traveling just to get a toothbrush had already tired him, but Xiaoshu's father insisted. Xiaoshu had little choice but to start the journey.

When Xiaoshu got on the bus and was about to close his eyes to rest, He saw an old man with a hunchback, who was holding a cane in one hand and carrying a big bag on his back. There was no open seat for him on the crowded bus, so Xiaoshu stood up–although he was very tired–to offer his seat to him. But the old man said,

"It's okay. You young men need to do tiring work, so please remain seated. I need to stand to strengthen my legs anyway." The bus driver suddenly hit the brake hard, and the old man almost fell. Still, he insisted on not taking Xiaoshu's seat. His cultivation earned Xiaoshu's secret admiration. Xiaoshu said

子，但是去附近的超商、大賣場四處找都找不到，網路也搜尋不著。爺爺說，那是以前老家附近的雜貨店才有得買，這下糟了，要跑好遠！

小樹算算時間，先搭公車再換乘長途客運，估計超過五個鐘頭的車程，才會到爺爺的家，光想就覺得累，還只是為了一支牙刷。但爸爸很孝順，讓小樹不得不回鄉下一趟。

當小樹搭上公車，想閉眼休息片刻時，微睜著的眼卻瞄見有位傴僂著身子的老者，一手拿拐杖，還揹著個大包，擁擠的公車上已沒座位了，小樹雖然很疲倦，但還是站起來讓位，老人卻說：

「沒關係，你們年輕人還要工作，很累，我們也要鍛鍊站的腿力。」車子忽然地緊急煞車，老人家差點跌倒，但他仍然堅持不坐。這麼有修養的長輩，讓小樹暗

to him, "I'm getting off, so please have a seat." He thanked Xiaoshu profusely before sitting down.

Therefore, Xiaoshu got off the bus before reaching his intended stop. The next bus would arrive in 20 minutes, so he waited in the bus shelter. A man in a wheelchair rolled to him. He was selling rags, toothbrushes, and toilet paper. Xiaoshu quickly glanced at his offerings, and Xiaoshu couldn't believe what he saw: the toothbrush that Xiaoshu's grandfather wanted. Xiaoshu was thrilled.

Xiaoshu asked him where he got those toothbrushes, and he said, "It's a manufacturer in the countryside, but they don't make them anymore. They gave me their remaining stock, so I am selling them for cheap." Xiaoshu was overjoyed. Xiaoshu paid for the purchase and left him with some extra change. He had just saved Xiaoshu from a long trip down south. Even if Xiaoshu had traveled to Xiaoshu's grandfather's house, there was no guarantee that he would be able to find and buy the toothbrush. Xiaoshu was very grateful for this series of events. Luckily, he had offered his seat on the bus to that man, which led Xiaoshu to get off the bus at that lucky bus stop where that disabled man happened to be selling the toothbrush he was looking to buy.

暗佩服。「我要下車了，你就坐坐吧！」聽小樹這麼說，老先生才一再致謝地坐下。

　　也因此，小樹只好提前下車，看看下班車還要等二十分鐘，就坐在候車亭等候。這時一位坐輪椅的身障者靠了過來，要推銷抹布、牙刷、衛生紙，小樹瞄了一下他推車上的東西，沒想到，居然裡面有一支跟爺爺一樣的牙刷，真是喜出望外！

　　小樹問他哪裡可以買到，「是一個鄉下的製造商，他們已經不生產這種牙刷了，所以這是存貨，送給我便宜賣。」小樹開心極了，買了之後還多給了些零錢，說不用找了，因為這給小樹省下了許多時間，如果真的到了爺爺家附近，恐怕還不一定能買得到呢。小樹很感謝，還好有讓位給老伯伯，他提早下車才會碰到這個身障者，也才有機會買到爺爺需要的牙刷。

This series of coincidences was really beyond belief. Long story short, Xiaoshu went home with the mission nicely accomplished in less than one hour.

A few weeks later, Xiaoshu's father said that Xiaoshu's grandfather couldn't sleep at night because another good friend in his hometown had passed away. Furthermore, he was still anxious and irritable because he couldn't find things; he was gloomy and wanted to go back to his own house. Then when he couldn't find things, he began to suspect that someone had stolen them from him. Xiaoshu's father started to be a little less patient with him and asked Xiaoshu to research and find a specialist who could take care of Xiaoshu's grandfather.

Xiaoshu searched the Internet for the symptoms of chronic anxiety. Most patients with mild anxiety disorders have symptoms like palpitations, chest tightness, or pain, often accompanied by racing heartbeat and general fatigue. It is the result of a need for others to see and feel one's fear, anger, guilt, frustration, sadness, loneliness, and so forth. It may come with sleep disorders such as insomnia and nightmares, as well as hand tremors, loss of appetite, dizziness, and, in severe cases, even negative feelings of near-death. These symptoms interact with one another and the result is a vicious cycle that

這一連串巧合真是太不可思議了，任務完成，小樹花不到一小時就可以打道回府。

　　沒隔幾週，爸爸說爺爺晚上都睡不著，因為聽說老家又走了一個好朋友，而且他還是常為找不到東西而焦慮、煩躁，成天苦著個臉，想回家。到最後，東西不見了，爺爺開始懷疑有人偷。這時爸爸有些不耐煩了，要小樹去找專家，好帶爺爺去看病吃藥。

　　小樹搜尋網路，想知道慢性焦慮到底會有什麼症狀：大部分輕度焦慮症患者，症狀包括心悸、胸悶、心悸或疼痛等，往往伴隨著心跳加速、全身疲乏等現象。那是恐懼、憤怒、愧疚、挫折、悲傷、孤獨等情緒孤兒，需要別人看見與感受。還可能伴隨著失眠、惡夢等睡眠障礙，以及手抖、食慾減退、頭暈眼花，嚴重時甚至可能出現瀕死的負面感受。這些症狀相互作用形成惡性循

affects the physical and mental health of patients of anxiety disorders. Their sensitivity to external stimuli makes them prone to negative situations such as excessive worry, unstable sleep quality, decreased concentration, and impaired memory. Furthermore, anxiety may lead the autonomic nervous system to be out of control, causing symptoms such as tightness in the shoulder and neck, headaches, and chest tightness, which are all part of the body's response to stress and anxiety to raise alertness to possible threats.

In short, anxiety is proof that you are trying very hard to hold on to your life!

"Xiaoshu's grandfather wants to prove that he matters, right?" Xiaoshu thought to himself. So he called cousin Smiling Anli, a counselor, and she suggested that Xiaoshu's grandfather should see a shrink first.

So Xiaoshu took his grandfather to see one, who, after running many tests, thought that the grandfather had anxiety disorders and, in order to relax, needed family members to accompany him.

After getting the medication, Xiaoshu considered taking one week off to accompany his grandfather. Just then volunteer team leader Wu called to invite Xiaoshu to help deliver some

環，影響焦慮症患者的身心健康。由於對外部刺激的敏感，使他們容易陷入過度擔憂、睡眠質量不穩定、注意力下降、記憶力受損等負面狀況。此外，焦慮的狀態下，自主神經系統也可能出現失調，引發肩頸緊繃、頭痛、胸悶等症狀，這些都是身體應對壓力和焦慮情況的反應，目的是提高警覺性以因應可能的威脅。

總之，焦慮，是你努力撐住自己生命的證明！

「爺爺想要證明自己的存在感吧？網路常說的刷存在感。」小樹想，於是打電話給諮商師微笑安莉表姊，她建議，還是先去看身心科醫生。

小樹帶爺爺去看醫師了，還做了許多測試，醫師認為老人家有焦慮症，需要家屬陪伴，才能讓他放鬆心情。

領了藥的小樹思量著，是否要請假一星期陪陪爺爺呢？剛好志工吳小隊長打電話來，邀小樹一起幫忙搬運

heavier assistive devices to the elderly.

Along the way, Wu said, "Now we have an aging population. In the absence of migrant domestic caregivers, when older people get sick, the younger generations invariably become caregivers, which inevitably means that some members of the family have to quit their jobs and lose their income. Even if the family can afford to pay the person who has quit their job–by sharing the cost among brothers and sisters, the person who quit their job will face difficulties returning to the workforce after a long absence. Furthermore, everyone, including the elderly, is idiosyncratic in some way, so taking care of the elderly is quite challenging. So how to help the elderly take care of themselves is very important." Xiaoshu nodded in agreement.

When they reached their destination, Xiaoshu saw a small community of two-story buildings with a garden full of flowers and plants. The two of them walked on a very beautiful path before entering a hall, where many silver-haired people were tentatively engaged in whatever they were doing. Some of them were repairing electric fans or bicycles, and some were sorting PET bottles, metal cans, glass jars, and paper for recycling. Whatever they were doing, everyone had a smile on their face.

一些較重的輔具給高齡長輩。

　　一路上，小隊長説：「現在已進入高齡社會，當長輩臥病沒有外籍移工時，如果都由晚輩照顧，家中人口單薄的就難免有人必須辭職全日照顧，即使有兄弟姊妹合力支薪給照顧者，日久這個人也很難再回歸社會工作，況且長輩都有個人的習慣，所以如何讓老者自己照顧自己是很重要的課題。」小樹點頭表示同意。

　　下車時，小樹看到一座二層樓的小小社區，庭園種滿了花草，走過很漂亮的小徑，進去大廳，好多銀髮族，都各自認真地埋頭工作，有人修理電風扇，有人修腳踏車，還有人回收寶特瓶、鐵罐、玻璃罐、紙張等，人人

The bulletin board on the wall reads: Cultural and Recreational Activity Schedule listing classes for fitness exercises, singing, sign language, calligraphy, painting, and others.

Xiaoshu and Wu walked by the infirmary, rooms for acupuncture, massage, rehabilitation, and reading as well as a prayer room and a small Buddha hall before they came to a warehouse. They worked together to move out the bed frame and auxiliary frame, and carried them into the car one by one, Xiaoshu asked Wu, "All those rooms for various purposes are roomy and comfortable. Are they all for the use of the elderly?"

A center staffer said, "Yes, this is a pilot area for long-term care, and all the funds are underwritten by entrepreneurs. The pilot has been going on for two years, and nearly 100 older people have gone through the pilot project, which is quite successful. Because this is a work of love, people here cherish resources and recycle valuable materials. They don't waste. In addition, the elderly also want to find their sense of value. They love others. Indeed, recycling and refurbishing old things makes the elderly feel that they, too, are being recycled to be contributing members of society again. This helps them lower their anxiety, so everyone is happy. Because of the opportunities for interpersonal interaction and self-realization,

臉上都掛著笑。牆上的公佈欄寫著：文康活動時間。還可見課表上有健身運動、唱歌、手語、毛筆字、畫畫等課程。

小樹與小隊長經過醫務室、針灸室、推拿室、復健部以及祈禱室、小佛堂、閱讀室，來到倉庫，他們合力搬出了床架與輔助架，一一抬上車，小樹很好奇地問，剛才經過這麼多不同的使用空間，又大又舒適，那都是給銀髮族使用的嗎？

「是，這是長照試辦區，所有的經費都由企業家捐助。已試辦兩年，有近百名長輩來過這裡，還算成功，因為這是愛地球的工作，愛惜物命，回收可用的資源，不浪費。而且高齡者也希望在工作中找到自己的價值感、發揮愛心。確實，回收整修舊物，讓老人也感覺到自己也被回收了，他們還是可再為社會所用，減輕了焦慮感，所以人人都很開心。」承辦人員一一解釋：「因

the elderly have stepped out of their comfort zone and out of the shackles of their fear and worry."

Then they were met by the sweet aroma of baking and pastries. A few elderly people were kneading dough and enjoying themselves in the large open kitchen. The staffer said, "Here they start work at 8 o'clock in the morning, and they have to stand up and stretch every half an hour. They sing together at 10 and they finish their work at 12 when they will pray and give gratitude and blessing together." With their own labor, the elderly earn their pay, which includes going under the tree to drink free tea, chat and make friends, and have a free lunch. The most important thing is that they feel that they are useful once again."

Wu said: "This is much healthier than health clubs. More than the food and drinks, the elderly are having fun and also regaining health and self-confidence. It's great. Let us know if you guys need help. We're ready to help."

Xiaoshu saw an old man cheerfully repairing a bicycle. Others were either repairing electric cookers or sorting out toys. "Is it hard work to do the repair?" Xiaoshu asked that man, who said, "What work? It's all fun. I am thankful for being able to come here every day. This is a job that I've loved

為有人際往來與自我實現的機會，長輩們都走出了舒適圈，也脫離畏懼、擔憂的框架。」

這時空氣中傳來糕餅香味，有幾個老人家在揉麵團呢，十分享受這裡開放式的大廚房，「這裡早上八點開始工作，做環保的規定每半小時要站起來活動筋骨，兩個鐘頭後合唱，四個鐘頭結束後還會一起祈禱、感恩與祝福。長輩們以勞力換取報酬，就是可以到樹下喝免費的茶、聊天交朋友，還有午餐也免錢。」承辦人滔滔不絕繼續說：「最重要的是，感受到自己是有用的人。」

小隊長說：「這比俱樂部健康多了，不是只吃吃喝喝開心，這裡可以養生、可以找回自信心。很棒，有什麼需要我們都願意來幫忙。」

小樹看到一位伯伯很開心地在修腳踏車，旁邊的人或者修電鍋、或是整理玩具，「修理這件事辛苦嗎？」「很好玩喔！每天能來這裡都很感謝。因為這是我從小

since I was a kid. It's nice to work here disassembling toys and putting them back together. It's wonderful to work here."

"Isn't that the same as not retiring?" Wu asked.

The staffer said, "Retirement means that you don't need to sacrifice today for the imaginary benefit tomorrow, that you don't need to sacrifice today to make money to support yourself. As long as you live in the present moment, live every day to its fullest, and do what you feel is fun, life has no pain and no pressure. Work for fun, do what you love, and you will feel happy. This is our purpose." That sounds reasonable. The staffer added that the repaired items here will be sent to remote areas to disadvantaged families, or sold to second-hand houses, and the proceeds will be used to support the operation of the center.

Xiaoshu saw rows of electric fans waiting to be repaired. Only at that moment did it dawn on him that his grandfather used to be a plumber, and he just might be able to find fun here.

When he got home, he saw that his grandfather was repairing an oven which he had procured from God knows where. Xiaoshu happily told him what he had just seen, and

就喜歡的工作，把玩具拆了又裝，在這兒工作真好。」

這樣不是跟沒退休沒兩樣？承辦人員回答小隊長的疑問：「退休就是不用為了想像中的明天而犧牲今天，為了賺錢養活自己而犧牲今天，只要活在當下，過好每一天，做自己覺得好玩的事，不是痛苦，不是壓力，工作都是為了好玩，做自己愛的事，會感到幸福愉快，這是我們的宗旨。」聽來還頗有道理。承辦人員補充，而且這裡修好的物品會送去偏遠地區給弱勢人家，或者賣給二手屋，收到的錢則回饋當做經費。

小樹看到好多台待修的電風扇沿著牆排排站，突然感應到爺爺，他以前是做水電工程的，應該可以來這裡找到樂趣。

回到家，看到爺爺居然不知哪裡搬來一台烤箱正在修理，小樹很高興地把剛才看到的告訴他，答應要帶爺

promised to take him to a place where he would definitely be very happy.

From this day on, every morning Xiaoshu's father drove Xiaoshu's grandfather to the environmental protection recycling workstation, and Xiaoshu's grandfather became happier and happier. Like a child, he couldn't wait to put on his clothes and shoes and get himself ready to go out of the house in the morning, and when he came home at night, he was tired and sweaty, but he was smiling.

Steady social activities and good interaction with family and friends can help reduce the incidence of anxiety disorders. Xiaoshu's grandfather did not need to be accompanied by his children or grandchildren, and he finally found a home in the long-term care center that has cured his anxiety disorder and delayed his aging. This incident has finally convinced Xiaoshu that as long as he learns and grows and follows the principle of altruism, his body, mind, and spirit are absolutely one and the same.

爺去他肯定會很開心的地方。

　　從這天起，每天早上爸爸都開車順路送爺爺去環保回收工作站，爺爺愈來愈開心，像孩子般，時間沒到就迫不及待衣服鞋子穿好了準備出門，晚上回家時雖然累得滿身是汗也都滿臉笑容。

　　醫師說，穩定的社交活動，並且與家人朋友保持良好互動，有助於降低焦慮症的發病機率。爺爺不用子孫們陪伴，在長照區終於找到了歸宿，治癒了焦慮症，相信也有延緩老化的功能，這個事件讓小樹終於相信，只要是學習成長，以利他為原則，身心靈絕對是合一的。

The Magic of A Positive Attitude

The elderly should always remember to be a role model for
young people.
Recognize that when old ideas are changed, it is an
opportunity for learning and growth.
Take a deep breath and ensure that you walk the talk.
Happiness takes a long time to cultivate, and it only takes
seconds to ruin it.
Anxiety is proof that you are trying to hold on to life.

正能量的磁場效應

年長者，隨時謹記當年輕人的榜樣

認知舊觀念的改變，是學習與成長的機會

深吸一口氣，確認你要講的話，也是你要做的行為

快樂需培養很久，想不開只要十秒鐘

焦慮，是你努力撐住生命的證明

吸毒一次，貽害一世

　　吸毒一次要終身戒毒，一個人吸毒全家受害。

　　吸毒人的錢的來源有：20% 是搶來的，45% 是販毒的，17% 是賣淫的，12% 是盜竊的；換言之，有 94% 都是經由犯罪活動而來。而吸毒人為什麼吸毒？有 38% 因為好奇，12% 親友疏離，26% 精神空虛，26% 追求時髦，24% 引誘上鉤。這麼多驚人的數字展現在你的眼前，你是否也感到了一種前所未有的恐懼呢？

　　據我個人的經驗，毒品的危害，後遺症是一輩子沒有辦法恢復。只是年輕時吸食毒品，因為身體還硬朗，所以一時感覺不出有什麼異常；等到年紀大了，慢慢地一些後遺症就會呈現出來。

我本身曾經在一九八七年的時候染上甲基安非他命的毒品惡習。安非他命是中樞神經的興奮劑，吸食安非他命之後會造成記憶體受損，產生出幻聽，幻覺，幻想。我曾經把家裡的摩托車牽到我的房間，因為使用甲基安非他命過量，產生出幻想症，幻想我是一個機車行老闆，所以我把摩托車牽到房間把它拆解掉。

　　隨著服用毒品日久，人的記憶體就會受損，而且這種傷害是一輩子沒有辦法回復的，如果沒有即時戒掉，最後會造成腦部萎縮、行為呆滯。

　　一旦染上毒品，就會一直尋求更刺激的感覺。我在二○○一年染上一級毒品海洛因（俗稱四號仔）。

　　海洛因是中樞神經的抑制劑。使用初期有興奮及欣快感，但隨之而來是陷入困倦狀態。具高度心理及生理依賴性，長期使用後停藥會發生渴求藥物、不安、打呵欠、流淚、流汗、流鼻水、盜汗、失眠、厭食、腹瀉、噁心、嘔吐、肌肉疼痛等戒斷症狀。副作用包括呼吸抑制、噁心、嘔吐、眩暈、精神恍惚、焦慮、搔癢、麻疹、便祕、膽管痙攣、尿液滯留、血壓降低等。部分病人會產生胡言亂語、失去方向感、運動不協調、失去性慾或性能力等現象。其毒性為嗎啡的十倍，濫用者常因共用針頭注射毒品或使用不潔之針頭，而感染愛滋病、病毒性肝炎（B 或 C 型肝炎）、心內膜炎、靜脈炎等疾病。在一九八〇年代因為共用針頭而染上 HIV 的人數暴增。大多數人放棄自己的人生，到最後往生的案例何其多！

　　我曾經有一棟屬於自己的三樓透天厝。因為染上了一級毒品海洛因之後，所有的家當還有房子全部都變賣掉，最後還淪落到偷拐搶騙。現在社會上詐騙猖獗，有一部分也是因為毒品泛濫所導致。

　　注射海洛因除了毒品的危害，還有可能因注射引發細菌感染。一旦被細菌感染，嚴重可能導致全身癱瘓，終身臥床。我們現在輔導的個案中，平均每百人就有三位是因為注射毒品感染而終生癱瘓。

　　這幾年一些新興的毒品越來越多。

　　K 他命，俗稱凱他命，三級毒品。是作用在中樞神經的麻醉劑，價格便宜、市面上容易取得，長期使用會造成膀胱纖維化萎縮、甚至大腦萎縮。

　　我曾經染上一級毒品海洛因，為了要把海洛因戒掉，所以找了替代品就是三級毒品 K 他命。我整整吸食兩個多月，結果造成膀胱纖維化、甚至血尿。人家說「拉K一時，尿布一世！」真的不是危言聳聽。我曾經輔導過一個個案，拉K的時間大概是三年，結果他整個膀胱纖維化，無法忍尿，因為上廁所脫褲子會來不及，往往就尿在褲子上，最後甚至在家都沒穿褲子，或包尿布。即使把K他命戒掉，也只會慢慢恢復，但絕對沒辦法恢復到原本健康的狀態。

所有的毒品危害都是一輩子沒有辦法恢復的。

「合成卡西酮」，又稱喵喵，三級毒品。濫用率逐年飆升！據衛生福利部食品藥物管理署的統計，二〇一八年九月單月含合成卡西酮類的混合藥、海洛因及甲基安非他命，即高居毒品通報案件前三名。合成卡西酮為近年來成長最快的新興濫用毒品，通報案件從二〇一二年的 1,356 件，成長至二〇一七年的 63,266 件。

台灣社會居然還有人說要毒品除罪化！？

因為我曾經遭受過毒品的危害，了解其中的一些嚴重性，所以我個人絕對反對毒品除罪化。為了我們的下一代，一定要堅決向毒品說「不」！

從學到覺的菩薩道上，最感恩今生原生家庭的母親不放棄的陪伴，及再生母親證嚴上人。屏東相信的力量監獄團隊還有高雄希望的力量監獄團隊，也在成就我的重生之路。深深感恩生命中的貴人，也期望能幫助更多的更生人！成為他們的貴人！

鐘炯元（更生人，反毒講師）

周圍都是您的貴人
Helpers All Around

作　　　者／林幸惠
英譯校訂／湯耀洋（YY Tang）
中文協力／蕭毅君、胡毋意
英文協力／張恭達、蘇錦俐
個案提供／朱曾美惠

發 行 人／王端正
合心精進長／姚仁祿
主 責 長／王志宏
叢書主編／蔡文村
叢書編輯／何祺婷
美術指導／邱宇陞
出 版 者／經典雜誌
財團法人慈濟傳播人文志業基金會
地　　　址／台北市北投區立德路二號
電　　　話／（02）2898-9991
劃撥帳號／19924552
戶　　　名／經典雜誌
製版印刷／禹利電子分色有限公司
經 銷 商／聯合發行股份有限公司
地　　　址／新北市新店區寶橋路 235 巷 6 弄 6 號 2 樓
電　　　話／（02）2917-8022
出版日期／2024 年 10 月初版
定　　　價／新台幣 350 元

周圍都是您的貴人 = Helpers all around /
林幸惠著. -- 初版. --
臺北市：經典雜誌，財團法人慈濟傳播人文志業基金會，2024.10
308 面；15*21 公分
中英對照
ISBN 978-626-7587-05-8（平裝）
　　1.CST: 人際關係 2.CST: 心理諮商 3.CST: 青少年成長
　　4.CST: 青少年輔導 5.CST: 青少年問題 6.CST: 反毒
863.59　　　　　　　　　　113014811

小樹系列

Little Trees